READ ME A
STORY, PLEASE

READ ME A STORY, PLEASE

Stories chosen by Wendy Cooling

Illustrated by Penny Dann

To Susan and Ann and their children
and grandchildren! *W.C.*

To J.D. with love *P.D.*

First published in Great Britain in 1998
by Orion Children's Books
a division of the Orion Publishing Group Ltd
Orion House
5 Upper St Martin's Lane
London WC2H 9EA

This collection © Orion Children's Books 1998
Illustrations copyright © Penny Dann 1998
Designed by Tracey Cunnell

A catalogue record for this book is available
from the British Library
Printed in Italy
ISBN 1 85881 548 7

CONTENTS

Say hello to Frog, Mouse and Duck! They have got together to tell each other their favourite stories – and you can listen too. Afterwards, they're going to have a picnic!

Did you know that **Frog** is too jumpy to sit still for long? He tells short hoppy **2 minute** stories.

Mouse likes to curl up cosily and tell stories that take about **5 minutes** each.

Duck does a lot of quacking, but in between she tells wonderful stories.

You will see Frog, Mouse and Duck at the beginning of each story,
and sometimes you'll find them hiding in the pictures,
or popping up to tell you something.

When you've listened to the stories, the picnic will begin,
and lots of friends will be there. You can see them all in the picture
at the end of the book.

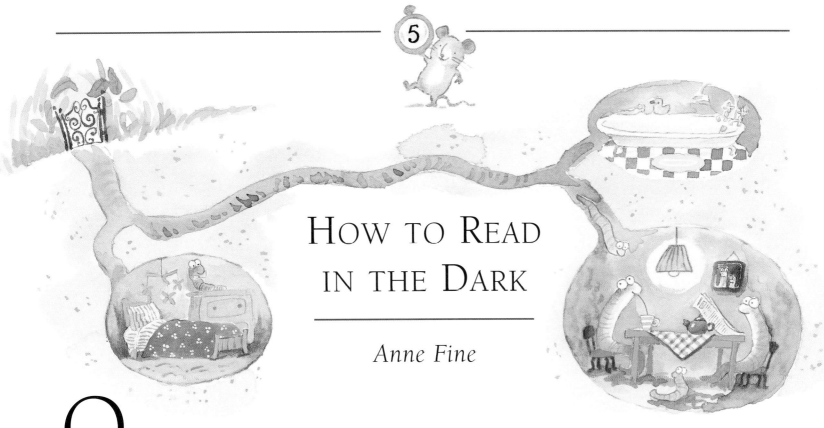

How to Read in the Dark

Anne Fine

Once upon a time there was a plain little grey worm called Hetty who wanted, more than anything in the world, to be a glow-worm.

"Don't be silly," said her father. "Glow-worms are *different*."

"It's no use thinking about it," said her mother.

But Hetty couldn't help thinking about it. She thought about it all the time. She imagined having a glow inside her, a glow she could turn on and off like an electric light.

She could light the way home through the woods when it was dark. She could find things people had lost in murky corners. Best of all, she could read secretly in bed at night, without anyone catching her. She simply *longed* to be a glow-worm.

"Never mind," said her mother. "Come and have a cuddle."

"Never mind," said her father. "Have a gingerbread star."

But Hetty wasn't satisfied with cuddles and gingerbread stars. She wanted to be a glow-worm, and she'd be one, whatever they said. So she went out in the garden and sat on a flowerpot, thinking.

11

And when she had done enough thinking she slipped off her flowerpot and made her way quietly out of the garden, all the way through the woods till she reached Wise Woman's cottage.

Wise Woman was busy sorting seed boxes. "Take my advice," she said to Hetty. "Go home."

But Hetty wouldn't. Instead, she set off over the hills to the royal castle.

The queen was busy counting all her coins. "What you are looking for is magic," she said. "I only have money and power. Go and ask the wizard."

Hetty found the wizard at the top of the highest tower. He was busy petting and soothing his assistant. A spell had gone wrong, and all her paws had turned bright pink and purple. She was worse than upset. She was sulking. She wouldn't even go and fetch the spell book so he could turn her paws back to jet black again.

"You hold the wand," the wizard said to Hetty. "I'll fetch the spell book." And off he went, the cat tucked underneath his arm.

Hetty was left all alone. She was left all alone for a very long time. She was cold. She was bored. And she was very, very hungry.

She looked at the star at the end of the wizard's magic wand. It was golden and glowing, like freshly baked gingerbread. She sniffed. It smelt like gingerbread. She pressed. It felt like gingerbread. She licked. It tasted like gingerbread.

And she was very, very hungry indeed.

All of a sudden, before she even realized what she was doing, Hetty had gobbled up the star, whole, all in one go.

She was *horrified.* And she could hear the wizard coming back!

Now Hetty was foolish, and she was stubborn too. But she was not stupid. She knew, whenever you swallow something funny, you have to tell, and straight away.

"Excuse me," she told the wizard politely. "I have just gobbled up the star at the end of your wand, by mistake."

But the wizard did not hear what she said. He was too busy looking for the star at the end of his wand.

"Please," said Hetty again. "I have eaten the star off the end of your wand."

"Just a moment," said the wizard impatiently. "I cannot solve anybody's problems until I have found the star at the end of my wand."

Hetty burst into tears.

The cat stopped sulking to explain the problem to the wizard.

The wizard took it very well, considering. "Thank you for telling," he said to Hetty.

"It's always best to tell," agreed the cat. "And there are plenty more wand stars in the cupboard. We bake them twice a week, and put the magic filling in on Thursdays."

"So," Hetty said, "I am not poisoned?"

"Poisoned?" exclaimed the wizard. "Certainly not! What a rude suggestion! The worst that will happen to you is that you'll start to glow a bit, inside."

"Like a glow-worm?" asked Hetty, getting excited. "Like a *glow-worm?*"

"I'm afraid so," said the wizard.

"How long will it last?" asked Hetty.

"Till you grow up," said the wizard. "If you are frugal, and do not leave it on all night."

"Oh, bliss!" breathed Hetty. "Oh, joy!"

"We'd better take her home," observed the cat. "It's getting dark."

They all set off together. The cat wore boots.

On the way home, Hetty kept glowing in the gathering dusk. It was a bit embarrassing. She tried to distract the cat and the wizard by pointing out bits of the scenery . . . until she got the knack of switching on and off.

Just as they arrived at the garden gate, Hetty's father came out and called her in for supper.

"Goodbye," said the wizard. "It was nice to meet you, even though I never did find out what it was you wanted."

"I don't want anything," said Hetty. "I have everything I want."

And so she did. She lit the way home through the woods when it was dark. She found things people had lost in murky corners . . . and, best of all, she could read secretly in bed at night without anyone catching her.

And, since she was frugal and never left it on all night, it lasted till she was grown up.

Wonderful Woody

Patricia Cleveland-Peck

There was once a young fox called Woody.

He kept his room tidy and helped his mum in the house. He played with his little brothers and sisters and never got cross with them. He gave his dad a hand around the place without being asked. He ran errands for elderly foxes. In fact he was living proof that not all foxes are bad.

But even so, foxes do have a bad reputation.

It made Woody very sad. He decided he would change things. He would make everyone love foxes.

He started with the chickens. As soon as it

got dark he crept up to the chicken hut and very softly he began to sing a lullaby.

"Rock-a-bye chick-chick,
Shut your bright eye
and Woody will sing you a lullaby . . ."

16

The chickens woke up in a panic. Up went their hackles, out burst their cackles. "Go away, nasty fox. We don't like you."

They clucked and muttered, fussed and fluttered, until with a heavy heart poor Woody stole away. How could he make anyone like foxes if they didn't listen?

Over the hill he saw some lambs having a last skip before bedtime.

"Lambkins, let me tuck you up in bed," he called.

The lambs skipped and scrambled, jumped and gambolled, and with baaing and bleating they called the old ram.

He was not amused.

"Clear off," he bellowed, "before I thump you one."

"You don't understand," said Woody, "I don't want to harm them. I only want to be friends with them."

"Well, they don't want to be friends with you," replied the ram. "You've had too many of them for dinner."

Woody felt most indignant. "And me a vegetarian," he said to himself. "Well, almost . . ."

It was much harder to make anyone like foxes than he had imagined.

Then he saw the baby rabbits playing in the field below. He ran towards them.

"I've come to kiss you goodnight," he said.

The rabbits jumped and hopped, squeaked and stopped, and with giggles and wriggles THEY KISSED WOODY BACK!

However, the mother rabbits were scared.

"A fox!" they squealed. "Licking his lips and getting ready to eat our babies!" Tears fell from their big eyes. "Leave them alone, you cowardly brute."

Woody backed away. "I don't want to hurt them. Only to kiss them goodnight," he said. "You don't understand. No one understands."

Very sadly he set off back to the village. On the way he came across a band of young foxes.

"Come with us and have some fun, Woody," they called, seeing his miserable face. "We're going on a dustbin raid."

Woody heard their laughter as they began knocking dustbins over. Well, why not? he thought. No one likes foxes anyway.

So he joined in and they all went round kicking and lobbing, hurling and robbing, rooting and looting, mucking things about and chucking things about until the whole village was a complete mess.

But at the end Woody did not feel better. He felt worse. This was not the way to make people like foxes.

The young foxes ran off and Woody sat by the roadside thinking. Then he saw Mrs Hoot the owl coming along with all the animals who worked at night. Everybody liked Mrs Hoot. Maybe she could suggest something?

"People think foxes are sly and slippery," she said. "You've got to show them that's not always the case." She looked round and shook her head. "You could make a start by helping us to clean up the village."

So Woody washed and scrubbed, polished and rubbed, and the more he cleared up the more Woody cheered up. He liked working with his new friends.

The next day Woody had an idea. He would have a party and ask them all. So he put up notices.

Soon the animals began to arrive. Woody made them welcome. First he taught them to dance the foxtrot. Then they played foxhunting, a game something like hide-and-seek. Then they had tea.

Then Woody got up and told a few jokes:

Finally, as a going home present, everyone was given a smart pair of foxgloves.

Mrs Hoot and her family, the hens and the ducks, the rabbits and the sheep and all the animals agreed it was one of the best parties they had ever been to.

And while it would not be quite true to say that they went away loving all foxes, they did think that Woody was wonderful. And that was a start, wasn't it?

PLAYING PRINCESSES

Adèle Geras

One day at Ruth's house, Sophie's mum was talking, Ruth's mum was talking, and Sophie's baby sister, Jenny, was chewing a plastic brick. Sophie and Ruth were dressing up. They were playing princesses.

Ruth's dress was too long. It was made of flowered cotton. It was old and torn.

"My dress is made of red satin," said Ruth.

Sophie's dress was too long. It was made of striped cotton. It was old and torn.

"Mine is pink velvet," said Sophie.

The girls went into the garden.

"This is my palace garden," said Ruth. "There are flowers and fruit trees and a lake with fish."

"I've got a palace garden," said Sophie. "With trees and flowers and a lake with fish, and fountains and rabbits and swings."

"I've got a royal throne," said Ruth.

"Where?" said Sophie.

"Inside," said Ruth.

"Show me," said Sophie.

So they went inside.

Ruth sat down on the window seat in the breakfast room. There were old toys on the window seat. There were old magazines on the window seat.

"This is my throne," said Ruth. "My throne is made of shiny wood. I've got three soft, silky cushions to lean on. The cushions are pink and purple and blue."

"I've got a royal throne at home," said Sophie. "My throne is made of gold. There are drawers under the throne."

"What for?" asked Ruth.

"For blankets. I cover myself with them when it's cold."

"I've got blankets too," said Ruth.

"My throne has music," said Sophie. "You turn a knob in one of the legs and you can hear music."

"Mine has music too," said Ruth. "And a cupboard full of cakes."

"Yes, mine has a cupboard too," said Sophie. "For cakes and biscuits."

"Does your throne have curtains?" asked Ruth.

"Yes," said Sophie. "Blue curtains with stars on them. You just pull them round you and make it night time whenever you like."

"My curtains," said Ruth, "are green. When you pull them tight, you can pretend you're under the sea."

"My name is Griselda," said Sophie.

"My name is Esmeralda," said Ruth.

Sophie's mum came in.

"Time to go," she said.

"Already?" said Sophie and Ruth together.

Sophie took off her dress. She put on her coat.

"It's white fur," she said. "With a hood."

"'Bye, Sophie," said Ruth.

"Griselda," said Sophie.

"'Bye, Griselda," said Ruth.

"'Bye, Esmeralda," said Sophie.

"'Bye," said Ruth.

On the way home, it started to rain.

"Drip on the mat, please," said Sophie's mum as they opened the door. Sophie hung her coat over the pram handle to dry.

Sophie sat down on a wooden chair in the kitchen.

"Look at my royal throne, Mum," she said.

"Lovely," said Sophie's mum, putting Jenny into the high chair.

"It's made of gold," said Sophie, and she sighed. "Poor old Ruth."

"Why poor old Ruth?" asked Sophie's mum.

"Well," said Sophie, "*she* thinks *she's* got a royal throne, but hers is only an old window seat. *She's* just pretending."

THE TROLL'S STORY

Vivian French

Father Troll was warty and ugly and as tall as a church tower. Mother Troll was warty and ugly and as tall as a house. Little Troll was round and hairy and just as tall as you can reach with your hand stretched up high.

On Thursday afternoon Little Troll was wet. He was very wet indeed. As he came stomping in through the open front door he left a trail of water behind him.

"Little Troll!" said Mother Troll. "You're back! Are you all right? How did you get on? Did you do what Father told you?"

"Don't fuss, Mother," said Father Troll. "Of course he did what he was told. Can't you see he's all wet? He's been tossed in the river, just like I was when I was a lad. That's what happens to us trolls, you know. The Great Big Billy Goat Gruff tosses us into the river. It's our very own special story, and now Little Troll can say that he is a real proper troll, just like me. Little Troll, come and give your old dad a hug!"

Turn to page 78 for the Trolls' very own special story!

25

"ATCHOO!" sneezed Little Troll.

"Dear Little Troll," said Mother Troll, "we'd better get you dry before you catch cold." And she hurried off to fetch the big fluffy towel that was hanging ready by the fire.

Father Troll sat himself down in his big chair. "Tell us all about it," he said.

Little Troll wiped a drip off the end of his nose. "I was a very good boy," he said, "really I was. I hid under the bridge just exactly like you showed me, Papa."

"Well done, lad," said Father Troll.

"I hope it was the rickety rackety bridge," said Mother Troll as she wrapped Little Troll in the warm towel.

"Oh, it WAS!" said Little Troll. "It was ever so rickety rackety! And I heard the littlest Billy Goat Gruff going patter patter patter–"

"Just a minute!" said Father Troll. "You mean trip trap, trip trap, over the rickety rackety bridge!"

"Oh yes, Papa. He went trip trap, trip trap. And then I jumped out and I said,

Mother Troll smiled as she rubbed Little Troll dry. "What a clever Little Troll you are!"

Little Troll nodded. "And it was exactly like Papa said it would be. The Little Billy Goat Gruff told me that his brother was going to come over the bridge. He said his brother was bigger and tastier and I should eat him instead."

Father Troll patted Little Troll's head. "Good, good. That's what they always say."

"So I waited for the Middle-sized Billy Goat Gruff," said Little Troll. "I waited under the rickety rackety bridge, just exactly like you showed me, Papa. And the Middle-sized Billy Goat Gruff came patter patter—"

"No no!" said Father Troll. "You mean trip trap, trip trap!"

"Sorry, Papa. He went trip trap, trip trap, over the rickety rackety bridge. And then I jumped out and I said,

Mother Troll clapped her hands. "Such a clever little troll!"

"Yes, Mama," said Little Troll. "And then the Middle-sized Billy Goat Gruff told me that his brother was going to come over the bridge. He said his brother was bigger and tastier and I should eat him instead."

Father Troll stamped his feet. "Yes! Yes! That's what they always say!"

"So I waited for the Great Big Billy Goat Gruff," said Little Troll. "I waited under the rickety rackety bridge, and while I was waiting I put my little tiny tippy toe into the water."

"I never told you to do that, Little Troll!" said Father Troll.

"No, Papa. But I did, and the water was oooh! So cold! And then the Great Big Billy Goat Gruff came trip trap, trip trap–"

"You mean tramp tramp tramp!" said Father Troll.

"–He went tramp tramp tramp and then I jumped out and I said,

I'm a troll!
Fol de rol!
And I'll eat you for my dinner!

"HURRAH!" cheered Mother and Father Troll together.

"And then," said Little Troll, "that Great Big Billy Goat Gruff said he wasn't going to be eaten. He said he was going to toss me into the river–"

"AND HE DID!" shouted Mother and Father Troll, and they grabbed each other by the hairy hand and danced round and round Little Troll.

Little Troll stood up.

"NO HE DIDN'T!"

It was very quiet. Mother and Father Troll stared at Little Troll.

"What did you say?" whispered Mother Troll.

"You mean . . . you ate the Great Big Billy Goat Gruff for your dinner?" whispered Father Troll.

"No!" said Little Troll. "I thought about how cold and wet and nasty the river was. I didn't want to be tossed in, even though Father Troll says all trolls get tossed in the river. I just jumped out of the way and then Great Big Billy Goat Gruff fell in instead."

There was another silence.

"So . . . why are you all wet?" asked Mother Troll.

"Oh, the Great Big Billy Goat Gruff couldn't swim," said Little Troll. "So I had to jump in to help him. And he was very *very* pleased and he said he'd never toss any trolls off the rickety rackety bridge ever ever *ever* again." Little Troll unrolled himself from the towel. "Is my tea ready?"

THE CAT
AND THE MERMAID

Shirley Isherwood

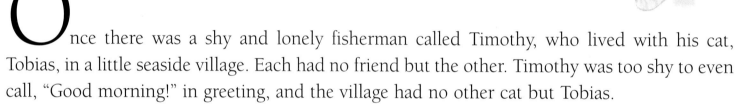

Once there was a shy and lonely fisherman called Timothy, who lived with his cat, Tobias, in a little seaside village. Each had no friend but the other. Timothy was too shy to even call, "Good morning!" in greeting, and the village had no other cat but Tobias.

Timothy had a flute made from a whale bone, which he had found many years ago on the beach. The music he played on this flute was very beautiful; sometimes it was sad and slow, sometimes as wild as the wind, sometimes happy. The villagers said, "Timothy speaks through his music!"

Every night, when the sea was calm, Timothy took Tobias out in the fishing boat. If the sea was rough, Timothy said, "Stay safe and warm in your basket, Tobias my friend."

Tobias's basket was made from wicker. It was very old, and creaked in a comforting way when he turned in his sleep. Inside the basket was a little soft quilt, sewn by the fisherman with big stitches, and big knots on the end of the thread, to stop the stitches from coming undone.

It was a wonderful place in which to sleep – but instead of staying in his basket when the sea was rough, Tobias crept through his cat-door in the kitchen. The villagers saw him go as silently as a shadow along the streets.

Tobias made his way to the clifftop where he sat all night, and waited for the fisherman's boat, *The Ariel*, to come safely home.

Often, by dawn, the sea had grown calm, and Tobias could hear the fisherman playing on his flute. Tobias sang to the music of the flute, as he sat on the clifftop. He did not sing well, but he sang with love.

Early one morning, as Timothy was making his way home, and Tobias was singing on the top of the cliff, they heard a voice they had never heard before – a most beautiful voice, like the voice of a bird or an angel. Even the rats who lived in the beached wreck heard it, and sat as still as rats made from stone, with only the tips of their whiskers twitching.

The next night, when Timothy and Tobias went out to sea, Timothy played on his whale-bone flute once more – and once more, the beautiful voice was heard. Looking down into the dark water, Timothy and Tobias saw a mermaid swimming by the side of the boat. Her long fair hair floated out behind her, and her tail flashed silver in the gentle waves.

She sang to the music of the flute. But when Timothy drew his boat up onto the beach, she turned with a powerful flick of her tail, and dived back under the sea.

That night, as Timothy and Tobias sat in their cottage, Timothy said, "If we could keep the mermaid with us always, she could be our friend. Every day I would play my whalebone flute for her, and every day we would hear her beautiful voice."

So he took one of his nets and hung it in a place where the rocks made an inland pool. Then he set out in his boat, with Tobias sitting in the prow.

When they were only just out of sight, Timothy took out his flute and began to play. Soon, the voice of the mermaid could be heard, as she came to the surface of the water, and swam beside the boat once more.

Timothy set sail for home, and the mermaid followed. When the boat reached the rocks which hid the inland pool, the mermaid swam on – but Timothy took his net and hung it from rock to rock so that once in the pool, the mermaid couldn't swim back out to sea.

That night, Tobias didn't hear the comforting, creaking sound of the wicker, as he turned in his basket. All he could hear was the sad voice of the mermaid, singing as she swam in her prison. The voice wasn't loud, but it could be heard in every corner of the cottage.

From above his head came the sound of the bedsprings creaking, as Timothy tossed and turned. Tobias left his basket, crept up to the bedroom, and tapped him gently on the cheek.

Timothy arose, went down to the kitchen, pulled on his great sea-boots, and put the whalebone flute in his pocket. Then he and Tobias made their way to the beach.

As they went, Tobias thought that he heard the sound of a baby crying, but there was nothing on the moonlit beach but sea wrack, seaweed, and sea creatures stranded in little pools which lay like mirrors in the sand.

When they reached the pool, Timothy sat down on a rock and began to play. But the mermaid didn't sing the music of the flute.

She clung to the net with her long white fingers, and gazed at Timothy and Tobias with her great dark eyes. Tobias thought that she was very beautiful and that he loved her very much.

After a while, Timothy put the flute back into his pocket, and he and Tobias made their way home. As they went, they heard the mermaid singing. The song she now sang was like a lullaby, and in the pauses of the music Tobias heard the voice of a mer-baby crying, "Mamma . . . Mamma . . ."

That night, when Timothy went out in his boat, Tobias sat on the cliff, even though the sea was calm. When *The Ariel* was out of sight, he began to sing. He sang a cat-song, and then the music of the flute, and the sad song which the mermaid sang, trapped behind the net.

Below him lay the wreck of the ship, and after a while, the ship's cat came padding up the cliff. He sat by Tobias's side, and joined in the song.

As the cats sang their duet, the rats came from their hiding places in the wreck. Tobias saw them creep up the cliff. They sat down some little way from him, and he saw their noses and whiskers twitch.

The rats listened to the song for a while, and then turned and scampered down the cliff, to where the net hung across the rocks. Tobias and the ship's cat went with them. Cats and rats sat on the rocks and sang. The words of the song said, "Let us free the mermaid. Let us gnaw through the net!"

From behind the net, the mermaid sang to her child, and the mer-baby sang in reply.

Far, far out to sea, the whales heard the songs. They too began to sing.

The music drifted through the streets of the village, and through the open bedroom windows. The sleeping villagers heard it in their dreams.

Timothy heard the music as he fished from *The Ariel*.

As he listened to the song he realized how cruel it would be to keep a mermaid from the sea and her child.

"When I return, I will free her," he said to himself.

On the rocks, the rats and the cats began to gnaw at the net. The mermaid lay in the water and watched them. From time to time she sang a snatch of song to her child, and her child sang back.

At last, the heavy net dropped into the pool, and the mermaid swam out to sea. Tobias watched her go. She was so beautiful and he loved her so much that he decided he would live beneath the sea with her for ever.

Down, down he went under the waves, following the silver tail of the mermaid. He saw fishes and sea-plants, and the mer-baby swimming to his mother. But he couldn't breathe, and knew then that a cat cannot live under the sea. He came up to the top of the water, and climbed onto a buoy, and waited. He saw *The Ariel* making her way home, and he heard the music of the flute. But even though he called and called, Timothy didn't hear him.

When Timothy reached the beach, he found the net lying in the pool, and the mermaid gone. He looked everywhere for Tobias, but couldn't find him. The only sign of him was the print of his paws on the rocks.

"Not only have I lost the mermaid, I have lost my dear cat," he thought, and went sadly home.

But that night, when he put out to sea, he heard the ringing of the bell, and when he sailed close he saw the mermaid and her mer-baby rocking the buoy to and fro. He saw too the figure of Tobias sitting on the top.

"Tobias!" he cried, and his cat leapt up onto the deck.

The mermaid and her mer-baby dived back beneath the waves.

35

"Wait!" cried Timothy, and he threw the whalebone flute to her. As it sank, it played music all of its own. Then, as he and Tobias began to make their way home, they heard once more the music which Timothy had so often played.

They heard too the song of the ship's cat as he sat on the clifftop, and the song of the rats, sitting once more in the wreck.

They heard, from far away, the song of the whales, and, from the shore, the song of the villagers drawn from their beds by the beautiful sounds, and who stood singing on the beach, to welcome back the fisherman and his cat.

Seeing this, Timothy and Tobias thought, "We have had good friends all the time!"

As they stepped from *The Ariel* the ship's cat came scampering down the cliff path to greet Tobias, and Timothy waved his hand to the villagers and called "Good morning!"

And as they made their way side by side up the beach, they found, lying in the sand, a bleached white bone, just right for making a flute.

HORRID HENRY

Francesca Simon

Henry was horrid.

Everyone said so, even his mother.

Henry threw food, Henry snatched, Henry pushed and shoved and pinched. Even his teddy avoided him when possible.

His parents despaired.

"What are we going to do about that horrid boy?" sighed Mum.

"How did two people as nice as us have such a horrid child?" sighed Dad.

When Horrid Henry's parents took Henry to school they walked behind him and pretended he was not theirs.

Children pointed at Henry and whispered to their parents, "That's Horrid Henry."

"He's the boy who threw my jacket in the mud."

"He's the boy who squashed Billy's beetle."

"He's the boy who . . ." Fill in whatever terrible deed you like. Horrid Henry was sure to have done it.

Horrid Henry had a younger brother. His name was Perfect Peter.

Better watch out – Horrid Henry's about!

Perfect Peter always said "please" and "thank you". Perfect Peter loved vegetables.

Perfect Peter always used a hankie and never, ever picked his nose.

"Why can't you be perfect like Peter?" said Henry's mum every day.

As usual, Henry pretended not to hear. He continued melting Peter's crayons on the radiator.

But Horrid Henry started to think.

"What if *I* were perfect?" thought Henry. "I wonder what would happen."

When Henry woke the next morning, he did not wake Peter by pouring water on Peter's head.

Peter did not scream.

This meant Henry's parents overslept and Henry and Peter were late for Cubs.

Henry was very happy.

Peter was very sad to be late for Cubs.

But because he was perfect, Peter did not whine or complain.

On the way to Cubs Henry did not squabble with Peter over who sat in front. He did not pinch Peter and he did not shove Peter.

Back home, when Perfect Peter built a castle, Henry did not knock it down. Instead, Henry sat on the sofa and read a book.

Mum and Dad ran into the room.

"It's awfully quiet in here," said Mum. "Are you being horrid, Henry?"

"No," said Henry.

"Peter, is Henry knocking your castle down?"

Peter longed to say "yes". But that would be a lie.

"No," said Peter.

He wondered why Henry was behaving so strangely.

"What are you doing, Henry?" said Dad.

"Reading a wonderful story about some super mice," said Henry.

Dad had never seen Henry read a book before. He checked to see if a comic was hidden inside.

There was no comic. Henry was actually reading a book.

"Hmmmmn," said Dad.

It was almost time for dinner. Henry was hungry and went into the kitchen where Dad was cooking.

But instead of shouting, "I'm starving! Where's my food?" Henry said, "Dad, you look tired. Can I help get supper ready?"

"Don't be horrid, Henry," said Dad, pouring peas into boiling water. Then he stopped.

"What did you say, Henry?" asked Dad.

"Can *I* help, Dad?" said Perfect Peter.

"I asked if you needed any help," said Henry.

"I asked first," said Peter.

"Henry will just make a mess," said Dad. "Peter, would you peel the carrots while I sit down for a moment?"

"Of course," said Perfect Peter.

Peter washed his spotless hands.

Peter put on his spotless apron.

Peter rolled up his spotless sleeves.

Peter waited for Henry to snatch the peeler. But Henry laid the table instead. Mum came into the kitchen.

"Smells good," she said. "Thank you, darling Peter, for laying the table. What a good boy you are."

Peter did not say anything.

"I laid the table, Mum," said Henry.

Mum stared at him.

"You?" said Mum.

"Me," said Henry.

"Why?" said Mum.

Henry smiled.

"To be helpful," he said.

"You've done something horrid, haven't you, Henry?" said Dad.

"No," said Henry. He tried to look sweet.

"I'll lay the table tomorrow," said Perfect Peter.

"Thank you, angel," said Mum.

"Dinner is ready," said Dad.

The family sat down at the table.

Dinner was spaghetti and meatballs with peas and carrots.

Henry ate his dinner with his knife and fork and spoon.

He did not throw peas at Peter and he did not slurp.

He did not chew with his mouth open and he did not slouch.

"Sit properly, Henry," said Dad.

"I am sitting properly," said Henry.

Dad looked up from his plate. He looked surprised.

"So you are," he said.

Perfect Peter could not eat. Why wasn't Henry throwing peas at him?

Peter's hand reached slowly for a pea.

When no one was looking, he flicked the pea at Henry.

"Ouch," said Henry.

"Don't be horrid, Henry," said Mum.

Henry reached for a fistful of peas. Then Henry remembered he was being perfect and stopped. Peter smiled and waited. But no peas bopped him on the head.

Perfect Peter did not understand. Where was the foot that always kicked him under the table?

Slowly, Peter stretched out his foot and kicked Henry.

"OUCH," said Henry.

"Don't be horrid, Henry," said Dad.

"But I . . ." said Henry, then stopped.

Henry's foot wanted to kick Perfect Peter round the block. Then Henry remembered he was being perfect and continued to eat.

41

"You're very quiet tonight, Henry," said Dad.

"The better to enjoy my lovely dinner," said Henry.

"Henry, where are your peas and carrots?" asked Mum.

"I ate them," said Henry. "They were delicious."

Mum looked on the floor. She looked under Henry's chair. She looked under his plate.

"You ate your peas and carrots?" said Mum slowly. She felt Henry's forehead.

"Are you feeling all right, Henry?"

"Yeah," said Horrid Henry. "I'm fine, thank you for asking," he added quickly.

Mum and Dad looked at each other. What was going on?

Then they looked at Henry.

"Henry, come here and let me give you a big kiss," said Mum. "You are a wonderful boy. Would you like a piece of fudge cake?"

Peter interrupted.

"No cake for me, thank you," said Peter. "I would rather have more vegetables."

Henry let himself be kissed. Oh my, it was hard work being perfect.

He smiled sweetly at Peter.

"I would love some cake, thank you," said Henry.

Perfect Peter could stand it no longer. He picked up his plate and aimed at Henry. Then Peter threw the spaghetti.

Henry ducked.

SPLAT!

Spaghetti landed on Mum's head. Tomato sauce trickled down her neck and down her new pink fuzzy jumper.

"PETER!!!!" yelled Mum and Dad.

"YOU HORRID BOY!" yelled Mum.

"GO TO YOUR ROOM!!" yelled Dad.

Perfect Peter burst into tears and ran to his room.

Mum wiped spaghetti off her face. She looked very funny.

Henry tried not to laugh. He squeezed his lips together tightly.

But it was no use. I am sorry to say that he could not stop a laugh escaping.

"It's not funny!" shouted Dad.

"Go to your room!" shouted Mum.

But Henry didn't care.

Who would have thought being perfect would be such fun?

FLOWERPOTAMUS

Michael Lawrence

There was once a hippopotamus called Gracie who was rather fat because she was about to give birth to a calf.

One fine spring day, Gracie wandered into a meadow full of flowers that dazzled and danced in the sunshine. She had never seen so many flowers, and she ran across the meadow, tumbling and rolling and rolling and tumbling through the bright spring flowers, over and over and over, all across the meadow, from end to end and back again.

Gracie liked it so much in the flower meadow that she didn't want to leave. So she didn't. For days, she stayed. For weeks. Tumbling and rolling and rolling and tumbling through the flowers to her heart's content.

Until the day her calf was born.

Gracie stared at her new calf in amazement. The new arrival was covered from head to tail in pink and red flowers. Gracie thought she was the most beautiful hippopotamus that had ever been born.

"I'll call you Poppy," she said, "after one of the brightest flowers in the meadow."

44

But there were some who did not think Poppy beautiful. They laughed at her.

"A hippopotamus covered in flowers?" the young hippopotamuses cried. "How ridiculous! How absurd! Whoever heard of such a thing? We have a better name for you. We'll call you FlowerPotamus!"

One day Poppy was sitting unhappily by the river wishing she wasn't covered in flowers. She didn't like being stared at and joked about. She didn't want to be different. She wanted to be like the others, not colourful, not covered in flowers, but grey and ordinary. Suddenly she heard a shout.

"Look, there's FlowerPotamus, admiring herself in the water!"

"Come on, we'll show her! Her and her fine flowery skin!"

Six young hippopotamuses charged at her. Poppy jumped up in fright and ran through a nearby gate. And there she found a meadow full to bursting with flowers that dazzled and danced in the sunshine. She raced across the meadow, and would have run out the other side, but the way was barred by a fence.

"Oh, what shall I *do*?" she cried. "Where can I *hide*?"

There was nothing for it but to wait for the others to catch her, and dance round her, and poke their usual fun. Poppy lay down among the flowers with a heavy sigh.

But then something very odd happened. The young hippopotamuses rushed into the meadow and . . . stopped. Looked about them, puzzled.

"Where did she go?"

"Is that her?"

"No, that's just flowers."

"Wait, I think I see her. Over there!"

"No, it's a trick of the light, she must have got out somehow."

Poppy realized that they couldn't see her in the flower-covered meadow because she too was covered in flowers! She looked like *part* of the meadow!

She lay quite still, hardly daring to breathe, and soon the others gave up and went away. Then, Poppy laughed out loud, and tumbled and rolled and rolled and tumbled through the bright spring flowers, over and over and over, all across the meadow, from end to end and back again.

From that day on, Poppy knew what to do when the other hippopotamuses chased her. She simply ran into a flower-covered meadow and lay down. It worked every time. They never saw her.

All through the spring she played this trick on them, and all through the summer too.

But then, one day, she ran into a meadow and the flowers were gone. Leaves were falling from the trees, but she couldn't hide among leaves. The other hippopotamuses caught her and made her life a misery.

With nowhere to hide, and no friend to talk to, Poppy became sad and lonely. Tears sprang from her eyes like enormous petals. This only made things worse. Now they laughed at her tears.

Winter came, and Poppy made up her mind to leave the herd. She knew that whatever she did, however friendly she was, the others would never treat her as one of them. She didn't belong there.

She travelled a long way, and as she travelled the skies darkened. Rain began to patter down. Thunder rumbled overhead. Lightning struck the trees. She took shelter in a cave.

Darkness closed about her and she was glad.

"I'll stay here for ever," she thought. "No one will laugh at me if they can't see me."

But then she heard a voice from deep in the deepest dark.

"Who's there?" said the voice. "What are you?"

Poppy's heart thumped.

"My name's Poppy, and I'm a hippopotamus."

"Oh," the other voice said gloomily. "Er, you're not thinking of stopping, are you?"

"Well, I *was*," Poppy replied.

"Hm! Well then, I'd better tell you that I'm a hippopotamus too."

"In that case," Poppy thought to herself, "it's a good thing it's so dark in here."

Weeks passed, and, though they could only just make one another out in the gloom, the two hippopotamuses began to get on rather well. Poppy sometimes wished they could go out into the light.

"But if we did," she thought, "he'd laugh at me, like all the others."

So they stayed inside, in the dark, all through the long winter months.

Gradually the light of spring reached into the cave, creeping a little further in each day, along the walls and floor and ceiling, until the darkness was no longer anything like as deep and black.

And when there was hardly any darkness left . . . they went outside and simply stared at one another.

"But you're just like me!" cried Poppy.

"And you're just like *me*!" cried the blue hippopotamus.

"When your mother was expecting you," Poppy said, "did she live in a meadow full of flowers?"

"Yes!" said the blue hippopotamus.

"And did the others laugh at you and poke fun so that in the end you ran away?"

"Yes!" said the blue hippopotamus.

"Well!" said Poppy.

"Yes!" said the blue hippopotamus. "And if I may say so . . ."

"Yes?" said Poppy.

"You're beautiful."

Now as it happened, just beyond the cave there lay a meadow full of flowers that dazzled and danced in the sunshine. The two hippopotamuses laughed out loud and they tumbled and rolled and rolled and tumbled through the bright spring flowers, over and over and over, all across the meadow, from end to end and back again. They never wanted to leave.

Time passed, and the two hippopotamuses produced calves of their own. And each calf, to their delight, was covered from head to tail in flowers.

Each spring the whole family would tumble through the meadow to their hearts' content, and if strangers came they simply lay down until they went away. No one laughed at the flower-covered hippopotamuses, no one made fun of them, no one chased them, because no one knew they were there.

Tool Trouble
at Smallbills Garage

Willy Smax

Benny the Breakdown Truck was watching Mike McCannick at work in Smallbills Garage. There were lots of cars to be repaired and Mike was rushing around trying to get them all fixed.

"Don't forget to check my brakes, young man," said Doris Minor.

"And while you're changing my oil," said Warren Beetle, who was up on the ramp, "you can adjust my clutch."

"Look at the mess he's making," said Francis Ford Popular, as Mike searched for the right spanner.

For once Benny had to agree with Mike's snooty old black car. "Yes," he said, "and it seems to be getting worse."

Alfie Romeo, the bright red sports car, was feeling impatient. "Hurry up, please," he said to Mike. "My carburettor is killing me."

"I'll be with you in a minute," said Mike, hunting around for his screwdriver.

Suddenly he tripped up over the wheel-brace and fell backwards over some oil cans. Mike's tools were scattered over the floor. He couldn't find anything.

"Oh dear," he said. "How can I ever get finished now?" He sat down sadly on an oil can and stared at the mess.

Francis Ford Popular looked snootier than ever. "I shouldn't have to put up with this," he said. "It's like living in a scrapyard."

"You've just given me an idea," said Benny. And he drove out of the garage and down the road to Brummingham.

By now the cars were starting to complain.

"I can't wait here all day with my bonnet up," said Alfie.

"I'm getting dizzy up on this ramp," said Warren.

"Please hurry up," said Doris Minor. "I'm getting awful twinges in my universal joints."

Poor Mike didn't know what to do. He looked around the garage and noticed that Benny was missing.

"Where's Benny?" he asked Francis.

"Here he comes now," said Francis. "And what on earth has he got with him?"

Hanging from Benny's tow-hook was a huge round metal object.

"Where have you been?" said Mike.

"I went to the scrapyard to borrow a giant magnet," said Benny. "Watch this!"

Benny lowered the big magnet. As if by magic, the tools began to roll across the floor. Then they jumped up and stuck to it.

"Oh, look!" said Mike. "There's my screwdriver! And there's my monkey wrench!"

Benny swung the big magnet around the garage until the floor was clear. When he had finished the magnet looked like an enormous hedgehog with all Mike's tools sticking to it.

"Thanks, Benny!" said Mike. "Now I can see my tools I'll be finished in no time."

He tightened up Doris's wheel-nuts. Then he reached for his screwdriver and adjusted Warren's clutch.

Soon Mike had fixed Alfie's carburettor. Smallbills Garage was peaceful again.

"That's better," said Francis, looking at all the tools sticking to the magnet. "I hate living in a mess."

"Well, now the tools are just like you," said Benny.

"Because they're clean and tidy?" asked Francis.

"No," said Benny. "Because they're stuck up!"

Toot, toot! Brmm, brmm! Benny to the rescue!

PIGGO AND THE PONY

Pam Ayres

Once, in a fold of the hills, there was a stately home called Badgerwood House. Families came to visit it, and play, and have picnics in its beautiful park. Behind the house was a Children's Farmyard, with lots of animals. One of the animals was a piglet. His name was Piggo.

One day Piggo was walking past the field where Edgar the big shire horse lived. He saw Edgar near the fence.

"Hello Edgar!" he called out happily.

"Hello Piggo," replied Edgar in a sad, gloomy voice. "Where are you off to?"

"I'm going home," answered Piggo.

"Oh," Edgar nodded, his eyes large and unhappy, "and who lives at your home, Piggo?"

Piggo thought. "My mum," he counted, "and all my brothers and sisters."

"Oh," Edgar said again, "your mum and all your brothers and sisters. That's nice."

"Why, Edgar?" Piggo asked him.

Edgar sighed a huge sigh down his soft pink nostrils and stared at the little piglet sadly.

"Look round my field," he told Piggo. "Who do you see?"

Piggo peered all round. "You, Edgar," he ventured.

"Any mum?" Edgar went on. "Any brothers or sisters? Anyone to say 'How are you, Edgar?' or 'Goodnight, Edgar' or 'See you in the morning, Edgar?'"

Piggo stared all round the empty field.

"No, Edgar," he said. "There's only you."

Edgar nodded. "I thought so," he replied, "there's only me."

He heaved another huge sigh, turned and plodded slowly away. Piggo stared after him, feeling very troubled. Poor Edgar was lonely.

Piggo heard footsteps coming and voices talking, so he hid, as he often did, behind an empty rabbit hutch on the grass.

Along came Clarence the Keeper, and Judy, who helped him when she wasn't at school. Their footsteps stopped. Piggo listened.

"Poor old Edgar," he heard Clarence say. "He doesn't look at all happy lately."

"No, he doesn't. I've noticed it as well. I wonder what's up?"

"He's lonely," Clarence told her. "Horses need friends just like we do."

Just then a group of children hurried along the path. They had come on a coach from school, and were very excited. Some stopped to look at Edgar, some ran on to the Adventure Playground and the steam train. Two teachers walked along behind them. They saw Clarence and stopped. One, a lady with long brown hair, spoke.

"Are you the Keeper?" she asked.

Clarence said he was.

"Good," she said, "then could you tell us where the pony rides are, please?"

Clarence said, "I'm sorry, but we don't have a pony. Edgar here gives rides in the farm wagon this afternoon."

"Oh." The lady sounded disappointed. "It was just that some of our children were hoping to have a proper ride, you know, with reins, and their feet in the stirrups."

Clarence said he was sorry again, and the teachers walked on.

"Come on, Judy," Clarence said urgently.

"Where are we going?" she asked, surprised.

"I'll tell you on the way. I've got a very good idea."

Piggo emerged from behind the rabbit hutch. "That sounded exciting," he thought as he trotted home. And it was.

A week later Edgar was lying down in his field when a blue horsebox was driven in. He got to his feet, interested, and walked over to investigate. Clarence climbed out of the Land Rover, let down the back of the horsebox and went inside. In a minute he came out leading what looked like a thick brown rug. On legs.

"Here you are, Edgar," said Clarence cheerfully, "this is Sherlock. He's a Shetland pony and he's come to give pony rides, and keep you company."

Clarence drove off. Edgar and the brown rug looked at each other. Edgar gave him a long, deep sniff.

"Hello, Sherlock," he said.

"Hello, Edgar," said Sherlock in a nervous little voice.

"You're very small," said Edgar.

"You're very big," replied Sherlock.

"And you're very hairy," Edgar remarked.

"That's because I come from a cold place," Sherlock answered.

"Oh," said Edgar, nodding.

"What's it like here? Are they kind?" asked Sherlock.

"Oh yes, very kind," Edgar assured him.

"I don't suppose they'll be kind to *me*," said the little pony sadly.

"Why ever not?" demanded Edgar.

"There's something the matter with me," whispered Sherlock.

"Oh no!" Edgar was dismayed. "What?"

Sherlock went on in a hushed voice. "It's called Outgrown. Everyone said it about me at my last home. They all said: '*Such* a nice little pony, what a pity he's Outgrown.'"

Edgar gave him a soft push with his nose.

"THAT isn't what it means!" he said indignantly.

"No?" enquired Sherlock hopefully.

"No," Edgar declared firmly. "Nothing of the kind. It means that whoever you belonged to before grew too big for you to carry, that's all!"

Sherlock gazed up in admiration. "Oh Edgar," he said. "Thank you. You are *very* clever."

"Well," said Edgar shyly, "I am a *bit*."

So that was how Sherlock came to live in Edgar's field. Sherlock gave all the children pony rides, and when Edgar passed by pulling the farm wagon they whinnied to each other in a friendly way. In the evening when their harness had been taken off, they would eat their supper and stand side by side in the field.

One night as Piggo was going home he heard Sherlock and Edgar in their stable, talking.

"Goodnight, Edgar," Sherlock was saying.

"Goodnight, Sherlock," said Edgar.

"See you in the morning," said Sherlock.

"Yes," said Edgar. "See you in the morning."

Piggo felt very pleased because he knew that his kind friend Edgar wasn't lonely any more.

LOTTIE'S LETTER

Gordon Snell

One day Lottie and Max heard a sad cry from the flower-bed:

"Yeeee-ow! Yeeee-ow!"

Among the flowers, they saw a little dog. Lottie picked it up. It held out a paw.

"Look!" said Max. "There's a piece of glass in it."

Lottie held the paw gently. She pulled the glass out, and said, "People shouldn't leave litter like that around. It's cruel."

"Someone should do something to stop it," said Max.

"We'll do something!" said Lottie. "We'll write a letter, and take it to the Queen of the World! People will listen if she tells them they're messing everything up."

"She won't take any notice of a letter from us," said Max.

"But she will if it's signed by the animals too!" said Lottie.

So they got a big piece of paper and Lottie wrote:

The world is precious, every bit – please don't make a mess of it.

She wrote her name, and Max wrote his. Then they got the dog to put a paw in some sticky mud, and stamp it on the paper.

Lottie
Max

Now Lottie's letter had a paw-mark.

They saw a pigeon with its beak stuck together with a piece of chewing-gum, so they took the chewing-gum out, and the pigeon put its claw in the mud and its mark on the piece of paper.

Now Lottie's letter had a paw-mark and a claw-mark.

Down came a seagull with its wings covered in oil spilt in the sea.

Lottie said, "You see, it's not just litter. There's all kinds of muck messing up the world." She got the seagull to put its wing on the letter.

Now Lottie's letter had a paw-mark, a claw-mark and a wing-mark.

They heard a bee buzzing around.

Lottie said, "If the flowers all die from fumes and pollution, bees won't be able to lick them and make honey."

They got the bee to make a mark with its sting.

Now Lottie's letter had a paw-mark, a claw-mark, a wing-mark and a sting-mark.

A frog hopped from the pond. It gulped fresh air, glad to be out of the slimy, dirty water. It put the mark of its long leg on the letter.

Now Lottie's letter had a paw-mark, a claw-mark, a wing-mark, a sting-mark and a leg-mark.

They saw a duck sitting by the pond. It stood up, and there underneath it was an egg.
"If the food they eat gets polluted," said Lottie, "eggs that ducks and other creatures lay won't hatch out." The duck rolled its egg over the letter.

Now Lottie's letter had a paw-mark, a claw-mark, a wing-mark, a sting-mark, a leg-mark and an egg-mark.

They walked by the river and saw a salmon.
"Look!" said Lottie. "The water's all mucky."
The salmon jumped out and rolled over on the letter, leaving the pattern of its scales there.

Now Lottie's letter had a paw-mark, a claw-mark, a wing-mark, a sting-mark, a leg-mark, an egg-mark and a scale-mark.

They came to the seashore and saw a dolphin jumping out of the sea.
Lottie said, "If the sea gets poisoned by nuclear waste, the dolphins will die."
The dolphin swam to the shore, dipped its tail in some sludgy sand, and slapped it down on the paper.

Now Lottie's letter had a paw-mark, a claw-mark, a wing-mark, a sting-mark, a leg-mark, an egg-mark, a scale-mark and a tail-mark.

"Is the letter finished?" asked Max.
"No!" said Lottie. "We need lots more marks. When all the other animals learn about the letter, they'll want to sign it too."

And they did.

There were tooth-marks from a lion and hoof-marks from a giraffe, and more paw-marks from a bear, and claw-marks from a parrot, and wing-marks, and sting-marks, and leg-marks, and egg-marks, and scale-marks, and tail-marks, and tooth-marks, and hoof-marks.

"Now the letter's finished," said Lottie.

"Shall we post it?" said Max.

"No," said Lottie, "we'll march with it."

Lottie and Max marched in front, and behind them came all the creatures who had put their marks on Lottie's letter.

The procession went on till it came to the Chair in the Air, where the Queen of the World sat, floating.

She said, "WISE! WONDERFUL! WELL DONE! I have never seen a letter with so many paw-marks, claw-marks, wing-marks, sting-marks, leg-marks, egg-marks, scale-marks, tail-marks, tooth-marks and hoof-marks."

"What will you do?" asked Lottie.

"I shall fly round the world with the letter," said the Queen, "and tell everyone to stop making such a muck and a muddle and a mess. Otherwise, the world may come to an end, and what will become of us all then?"

Lottie and Max gazed up as the Queen flew away to warn people, calling out,

"THE WORLD IS PRECIOUS, EVERY BIT –
PLEASE DON'T MAKE A MESS OF IT!"

"I hope all the people will listen," said Lottie.
And so do we all.

RORY, THE DEPLORABLY NOISY BABY

Paul and Emma Rogers

Smash! Crash! What was that? It sounded like an elephant stampeding through a supermarket! But it wasn't.

Toot! Toot! Beep! Beep! What was that? It sounded like angry drivers in a traffic jam! But it wasn't.

Cling! Clang! Jangle! Bash! Twang! What was that? It sounded like a bandstand collapsing and all the musicians with all their instruments crashing through it! But it wasn't.

No, all that noise was made by just one baby.

Little Rory Holler had spent the morning playing in the kitchen . . . in the garden . . . and at the piano . . .

And all that noise was nothing compared to Rory's voice. For Rory had the loudest, shrillest, shriekiest voice ever.

His laugh rattled the plates on the dresser. His cry sent birds flying out of the trees. When Rory opened his mouth wide, the cat put its paws in its ears. When Rory screamed, even the dog couldn't hear itself howl.

Rory's mum and dad put up with his noisiness at home, but taking him out wasn't so easy. Mrs Holler never had to queue in the shops. As soon as Rory started to shout, everyone moved aside and said, "After you." Poor Mrs Holler blushed as she whispered, "Hush, Rory, do."

The summer approached and Rory was six months old. The Hollers decided they needed a holiday.

Mrs Holler said,
"Let's fly to a sunny beach in Spain."
But Mr Holler said,
"What if he started to shout on the plane?"
They thought again.
After a while, Mr Holler said,
"Let's drive to that nice hotel we know."
But Mrs Holler shook her head.
"If Rory yelled, they'd ask us to go."
Surely there must be *something* they could do.
Yes! There was! They both thought of it at once.

Five weeks later, the Hollers poked cotton wool in their ears and set off by car for a lonely seaside cottage. It was the perfect place for Rory. He could bang and bellow and shout, and no one but his mum and dad could hear him.

On the second day, they took Rory to play by the sea. When they arrived on the beach, it only took one high-pitched screech and they had the sand to themselves . . .

On the third day, they walked around the harbour. Rory roared with delight at the sight of the boats.

"I feel so embarrassed!" said Mrs Holler, as people stared. "There's nowhere to hide!"

Mr Holler whispered in Rory's ear,

"Be a good boy, and we'll go for a ride."

Rory grinned, silently. The Hollers hurried round to the sign at the quayside that said:

The boat rocked gently as Mrs Holler climbed aboard. Mr Holler passed her first Rory, then a bag full of things to help keep him quiet – buns, books, a dummy, a teddy bear, a strip of sticking plaster. Some were to eat and some were to play with, and some could be stuffed into – or over – Rory's mouth if he started screaming.

But, to his mum's and dad's surprise, he didn't make a squeak. For a while he seemed quite entranced by the bobbing up and down of the boat and nearly nodded off to sleep. Then suddenly the engine started. Rory opened his mouth to yell, and at once it was filled with a large bun. By the time they were out of the harbour, they had already used all the buns and were trying to stop his screams with the dummy.

"I knew this would happen. We shouldn't have come!" said Mrs Holler. "Rory will spoil it for everyone."

But then, as the boat chugged out to sea, Rory's eyes began to close.

"What a relief! He's having a nap. If only he'd stay there, asleep on your lap," sighed Mr Holler.

The boat rocked gently. The baby slept. Then suddenly, the engine stopped. The skipper fumbled with rags and spanners but couldn't get it started. Everyone went quiet. All you could hear was the water lapping against the side of the boat and Rory snoring. As the wind blew them further and further out to sea, people were getting worried.

"We can't just sit here!"

"What can we do?"

"If someone could see us . . ."

"Yes, but who?"

There were no other boats in sight. The harbour was only a speck on the horizon.

At last a ship appeared in the distance. People waved coats and hankies, and the skipper waved a flag.

"AHOY!" one of them shouted.

Two or three others joined in.

But the skipper said, "Shouts aren't loud enough – nowhere near. There isn't a hope that they'll hear us from here."

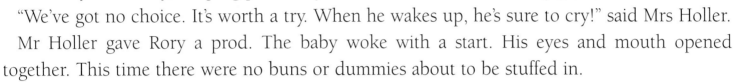

Mr Holler looked at his wife and said, "Should we, dear?"

There lay little Rory, sleeping peacefully.

"We've got no choice. It's worth a try. When he wakes up, he's sure to cry!" said Mrs Holler.

Mr Holler gave Rory a prod. The baby woke with a start. His eyes and mouth opened together. This time there were no buns or dummies about to be stuffed in.

The first sound was just a growl. The passengers looked around. Then it was a yell. The passengers shouted, "Louder! Louder! Keep him awake! Pinch him! Poke him! Give him a shake!"

Then Rory's yell exploded into an unbelievable, ear-splitting scream. The passengers fell silent. More and more the baby bawled. Had the ship in the distance turned? People stopped waving coats and hankies and put their fingers in their ears.

Rory's wailing was like a siren. Was the ship coming towards them? Yes! It was! Rory, the smallest passenger aboard, had saved them all!

The ship pulled alongside. The crew hauled them one by one to safety.

"Three cheers for the baby who's saved the day!" the skipper cried. "All together now – Hip Hip . . ."

But the "Hooray" was drowned by Rory's horrendous hollering!

"Bless my barnacles!" said the skipper. "Yes, well done! That's a mighty fine foghorn you have in your son!"

A few days later, back on land, a huge hall was packed with people. At the centre of the stage sat Rory, his two teeth stuck into a toffee apple.

"He's never going to keep quiet through this," said Mrs Holler. "I wish we'd given today a miss!"

"We are here," the mayor said, "to present this baby with a special award for amazing bravery!"

The mayor held up a medal on a coloured ribbon. Mr Holler held up Rory. He remained wonderfully quiet.

Then, just as the medal was being pinned onto his sailor suit, the pin pricked him. Rory dropped the toffee apple. His mouth flew open.

He shouted and screamed, he bawled and bellowed, he wailed and roared and hooted and howled.

"Say thank you, Rory," his father whispered in his ear.

But by the time Rory was quiet, there was no one to say thank you *to*.

Everyone but the Hollers had left the hall!

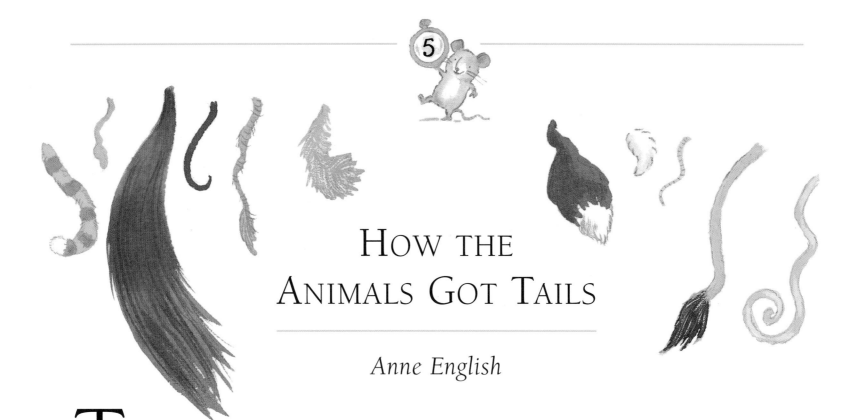

How the Animals Got Tails

Anne English

There once was a time when none of the animals in the world had tails – not a single one. The horse had no tail to swish away the flies. The dog had no tail to wag when he was happy. And the monkey had no tail to curl round the branches when he was jumping from tree to tree.

The wise lion, who was king of the animals, knew there was something missing, and he thought and thought until he had a clever idea.

"Animals, animals," he roared, "I, the lion, the king of all the animals, command you to come to a meeting in the Great Meadow. Roar, roar!"

When they heard the lion roar every animal from far and near came hurrying to the Great Meadow. First came the fox and the squirrel, then the horse, the dog and the cat. Then came the monkey and the mouse. The lion waited for them all to arrive.

"Sit in a circle round me," he told them, "and hear what I have to say."

More and more animals came until the circle was almost complete. The elephant and the pig were nearly late, but last of all was the rabbit. He had been eating a carrot when he heard the lion roar, and had finished it before coming to the Great Meadow. And now he was the very last to arrive.

The lion held up his paw for silence.

"Friends," he said, "I have been thinking." He paused. "I have been thinking that something is missing for all of us, so I have invented – TAILS." And he held up a huge bag full of tails.

"You will get one each," he told the animals, "and wear your own always." How the animals clapped and cheered their clever leader.

"Now, first come, first served," said the lion, "and as I was here first I get the first tail." And from the bag he pulled a marvellous long golden tail with a black tassel at the end, and put it on himself. How wonderful it made him look. He waved it proudly, while the animals watched, and waited for their tails.

The lion stood in the circle and called out, "The fox." He gave the fox a long, thick, bushy tail, like a brush. Fox put it on and went away proudly.

"Next, the squirrel," said the lion. And the squirrel too got a huge bushy tail, which he curved up over his back before leaping away. The horse came next, and from the bag the lion pulled a long, strong, black tail, combed out until it was silky and straight. The horse was delighted, and galloped off swishing his new tail from side to side.

The cat and the dog came into the circle together, and they each received a straight tail which would wave or wag from side to side, or up and down, as they pleased. The monkey was given an extremely long tail. He curled it over his arm, so that he couldn't trip over it, and went jumping away into the trees.

By now the bag of tails was half empty, so there was not much choice for the elephant when it came to his turn. In fact his tail looks like a piece of chewed string – just look at it, if you see an elephant. But he put it on quite happily, and lumbered off.

"Mouse," called the lion, and the mouse came. Now considering how small a mouse is, he did very well, for the tail pulled from the bag for him was very long indeed. Mouse put it on and scuttled away, trailing his tail behind him.

"Humph!" said the lion, as the pig came up. "Not much left now," and he took out yet another straight, stringy tail. The pig was not pleased.

"The elephant and the mouse have tails like that," he said. "Can I have something different, please?" The lion shook his head.

"Sorry," he said, "you arrived almost last, and this is all there is."

"Oh, very well then," said the pig, taking the stringy tail and looking at it crossly. "This will just not suit me," he muttered. "Just imagine a pig with a straight tail!"

As he walked away he trod on a thick twig.

"Hoink, hoink," he grunted, "I have an idea. Lions aren't the only ones with brains." And he took his tail and wrapped it tightly round the twig. When he pulled the twig out the tail stayed curly.

"I like that better," said the pig, and he stuck on his new curly tail.

Last of all to receive a tail was the rabbit. By now the lion was rather tired of tails, and he hurriedly shook the bag upside down to get out the last one. It was tiny – just a tiny thin piece of tail. The poor rabbit was disappointed, but he knew there was nothing left, so he thanked the lion and took the tail. But it was so small he couldn't bring himself to put it on.

"This is just a nothing tail," he told himself. "Not a bushy tail, like the fox's, or swishy like the horse's. Not even long enough to wave or wag. I will look silly with this one." He sighed. The lion had given them all tails, and they would have to wear them, the rabbit knew.

As the rabbit wandered along, thinking about his piece of tail, he came to a prickly bush, and *he* had a wonderful idea.

"Rabbits can think as well as lions and pigs," he said. And he took his tail and stroked it gently backwards and forwards over the prickles, until the tail became soft and round.

"That's better," thought the rabbit, looking at it happily. Then he stuck on his new fluffy tail, and bobbed away merrily.

A NAME FOR NETTIE

Lynda Britnell

One sunny morning a fairy was sitting under a nettle.

She wasn't an ordinary fairy. She had strap-on wings. She had spiky hair like a hedgehog. And she was very sad because she didn't have a name.

A worm came along the path and stopped by the fairy.

"What's your name?" he asked.

"I don't have a name," said the fairy.

"Oh dear. Well, Worm is a nice name. We could call you Worm," said the worm.

"No!" said the fairy. "I don't want to be called Worm. Worm is not the name for me."

So the worm went away.

Then a spider came down the path and stopped by the fairy.

"Hello," said the spider. "What's your name?"

"I don't have a name," said the fairy.

"Oh dear. Well, Spider is a nice name," said the spider. "We could call you that."

"No!" said the fairy. "I don't want to be called Spider. Spider is not the name for me."

So the spider walked on.

Next a caterpillar came down the path and stopped beside the fairy.

"Hello, what's your name?" asked the caterpillar.

"I don't have a name," said the fairy.

"Oh dear. Well, Caterpillar is a nice name. We could call you Caterpillar," said the caterpillar.

"No!" said the fairy. "I don't want to be called Caterpillar. Caterpillar is not the name for me."

So the caterpillar went on her way.

Finally, a gnome came down the path and stopped beside the fairy.

"You're a new fairy, aren't you?" said the gnome. "Have you got a name yet?"

"No I haven't," said the fairy. "And I don't want to be called Gnome!"

The gnome laughed. "My name isn't Gnome," he said. "It's Know-It-All, and I know how fairies are named. Fairies are named after flowers. Your first name comes from the plant you're found under, and your second name comes from a plant nearby."

"So what's my name?" said the fairy.

"Well, I found you under these nettles," said Know-It-All, "so, your first name is Nettle. And this plant here is mugwort. So your name is Nettle Mugwort."

"I think," said Nettle, "that I would rather be called Nettie Mugwort."

"Yes," said Know-It-All, "I think you are right."

Nettie danced round and round singing,

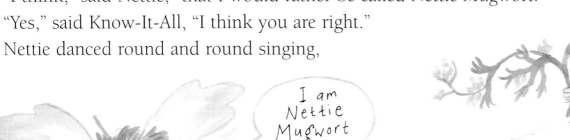

until she was quite dizzy.

When she stopped, Know-It-All said, "We can't leave you here on your own. Come with me and meet the other fairies."

Know-It-All held Nettie's hand and led her down the path and over a little bridge. Beside the river there were lots of fairies.

"Hello, this is Nettie Mugwort," said Know-It-All. "She's a new fairy."

"Hello, I'm Bluebell," said a fairy. "Come and sit with me, Nettie. We're going to have a picnic."

So Nettie and Know-It-All sat down with Bluebell and the other fairies.

And that is how Nettie Mugwort got her name and came to live in the fairy forest.

THE THREE BILLY GOATS GRUFF

Vivian French

A Great Big Billy Goat Gruff, a Middle-sized Billy Goat Gruff and a Little Billy Goat Gruff once lived in a green grassy field beside a stream. All day long the Little Billy Goat Gruff ate, and the Middle-sized Billy Goat Gruff ate and ate, and the Great Big Billy Goat Gruff ate and ate and ATE . . . until one day there was no grass left. Not so much as a leaf.

"Maa!" said the Little Billy Goat Gruff. "I'm hungry!"

"Maa!" said the Middle-sized Billy Goat Gruff. "I'm very hungry!"

"Maa! Maa! Maa!" said the Great Big Billy Goat Gruff.

"I'M VERY HUNGRY INDEED!"

"Whatever shall we do?" asked the Little Billy Goat Gruff.

"Whatever can we do?" asked the Middle-sized Billy Goat Gruff.

"I know what to do!" said the Great Big Billy Goat Gruff. "We must cross the rickety rackety bridge and go and live in the fine green grassy field on the other side of the stream!"

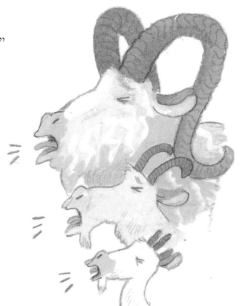

The Little Billy Goat Gruff went first. He pattered down the bare empty field. Then trip trap, trip trap! Over the rickety rackety bridge went the Little Billy Goat Gruff. Suddenly–

R R R R R R R R R R R R R R R R

a huge ugly troll jumped right into the middle of the bridge.

"Who's that trip trapping over my bridge?" he roared.

"Oh, Mr Troll – please don't eat me for your dinner!" said the Little Billy Goat Gruff. "I'm only a little billy goat, and I'm as thin as can be. Why don't you wait for my brother? He's much bigger and tastier than I am!"

The troll scratched his hairy ears. "Very well," he said. "Be on your way!" And the Little Billy Goat Gruff hopped and skipped and jumped off the rickety rackety bridge and into the fine green grassy field on the other side of the stream.

The Middle-sized Billy Goat Gruff came next. He trotted down the bare empty field. Then trip trap, trip trap! Over the rickety rackety bridge went the Middle-sized Billy Goat Gruff. Suddenly–

RRRRRRRRRRRRRR

the huge ugly troll jumped right into the middle of the bridge.

"Who's that trip trapping over my bridge?" he roared.

I'm a troll Fol de Rol! And I'll eat you for my dinner!

"Oh, Mr Troll – please don't eat me for your dinner!" said the Middle-sized Billy Goat Gruff. "I'm only a middle-sized billy goat, and I'm as thin as can be. Why don't you wait for my brother? He's much bigger and tastier than I am!"

The troll rubbed his warty nose. "Very well," he said. "Be on your way!" And the Middle-sized Billy Goat Gruff leapt and jumped off the rickety rackety bridge and into the fine green grassy field on the other side of the stream.

The Great Big Billy Goat Gruff came next. He stamped down the bare empty field. Then TRAMP! TRAMP! TRAMP! Over the rickety rackety bridge went the Great Big Billy Goat Gruff. Suddenly–

RRRRRRRRRRR

the huge ugly troll jumped right into the middle of the bridge.

"Who's that tramp tramp tramping over my bridge?" he roared.

"OH NO YOU'RE NOT!" bellowed the Great Big Billy Goat Gruff. He put his head down and he pawed the ground, and then he charged. He rushed at the troll, and he tossed him into the stream with a great big

Splashhhh!

Then the Great Big Billy Goat Gruff walked slowly off the rickety rackety bridge and into the fine green grassy meadow where his brothers were waiting for him. All three billy goats lived in the field for a long, long time, and they ate and ate and they ate until . . . they were all three Great Big Billy Goats Gruff!

THE STRANGE EGG

Margaret Mahy

Once Molly found a strange leathery egg in the swamp. She put it under Mrs Warm the broody hen to hatch it out. It hatched out into a sort of dragon.

Her father said, "This is no ordinary dragon. This is a dinosaur."

"What is a dinosaur?" asked Molly.

"Well," said her father, "a long time ago there were a lot of dinosaurs. They were all big lizards. Some of them were bigger than houses. They all died long ago . . . All except this one," he added gloomily. "I hope it is not one of the larger meat-eating lizards as then it might grow up to worry the sheep."

The dinosaur followed Mrs Warm about. She scratched about for worms for it, but the dinosaur liked plants better.

"Ah," said Molly's father. "It is a plant-eating dinosaur – one of the milder kind. They are stupid but good-natured," he added.

Professors of all ages came from near and far to see Molly's dinosaur. She led it around on a string. Every day she needed a longer piece of string. The dinosaur grew as big as ten elephants. It ate all the flowers in the garden and Molly's mother got cross.

"I am tired of having no garden and I am tired of making tea for all the professors," she said. "Let's send the dinosaur to the zoo."

"No," said Father. "The place wouldn't be the same without it."

So the dinosaur stayed. Mrs Warm used to perch on it every night. She had never before hatched such a grand successful egg.

One day it began to rain . . . It rained and rained and rained and rained so heavily that the water in the river got deep and overflowed.

"A flood, a flood – we will drown," screamed Molly's mother.

"Hush, dear," said Molly's father. "We will ride to a safe place on Molly's dinosaur. Whistle to him, Molly."

Molly whistled and the dinosaur came towards her with Mrs Warm the hen, wet and miserable, on his back. Molly and her father and mother climbed onto the dinosaur's back with her. They held an umbrella over themselves and had hot drinks out of a thermos flask. Just as they left, the house was swept away by the flood.

"Well, dear, there you are," said Molly's father. "You see it was useful to have a dinosaur, after all. And I am now able to tell you that this is the biggest kind of dinosaur and its name is Brontosaurus."

Molly was pleased to think her pet had such a long, dignified-sounding name. It matched him well. As they went along they rescued a lot of other people climbing trees and house tops, and floating on chicken crates and fruit boxes. They rescued cats and dogs, two horses and an elephant which was floating away from a circus. The dinosaur paddled on cheerfully. By the time they came in sight of dry land, his back was quite crowded. On the land policemen were getting boats ready to go looking for people, but all the people were safe on the dinosaur's back.

After the flood went down and everything was as it should be, a fine medal was given to Molly's dinosaur as most heroic animal of the year and many presents were given to him.

The biggest present of all was a great big swimming pool made of rubber so you could blow it up. It was so big it took one man nearly a year to blow it up. It was a good size for dinosaurs of the Brontosaurus type. He lived in the swimming pool after that (and Molly's mother was able to grow her flowers again). It is well known that Brontosauruses like to swim and paddle. It took the weight off his feet. Mrs Warm the hen used to swim with him a bit, and it is not very often you find a swimming hen.

So you see this story has a happy ending after all, which is not easy with a pet as big as ten elephants. And just to end the story I must tell you that though Molly's dinosaur had the long name of Brontosaurus, Molly always called him Rosie.

CROCODILE TEARS

Sue Inman

One day, Mrs Mumbles set off to feed the ducks at the park. But when she arrived at her favourite bench, she was surprised to find that somebody was already sitting there.

It was a gigantic crocodile, and this gigantic crocodile was crying great big huge enormous crocodile tears. It was very sad.

"Oh, you poor dear thing," said Mrs Mumbles. "Here, have a sweetie to make you feel better."

The gigantic crocodile gobbled up the sweet, but when he had finished, he started to cry again. This made Mrs Mumbles feel so sad that she sat down on the bench next to the gigantic crocodile and *she* began to cry too.

After a little while, a clown came along.

"Why are you crying?" said the clown to Mrs Mumbles, and Mrs Mumbles replied,

"I'm crying because this crocodile is crying and I can't make him stop."

"I expect I can," said the clown. "Watch this."

Then the clown did a very funny trick. The gigantic crocodile watched the trick, but when it was over, he started to cry again.

This made the clown so sad that he sat down on the bench next to Mrs Mumbles, and *he* started to cry too!

Soon a man with a fiddle happened to pass that way.

"Why are you crying?" said the fiddler to the clown, and the clown replied,

"I'm crying because this gigantic crocodile is crying and Mrs Mumbles can't make him stop, and neither can I."

"Oh," said the fiddler. "I expect I can cheer him up!" And he took out his fiddle and played a very jolly little tune on it.

The gigantic crocodile listened politely to the jolly little tune, but when it was over he started crying again. This made the fiddler so sad that he sat down on the bench next to the clown and started to cry too.

Just then a little girl called Lucy arrived with her mum.

"Why are you crying?" Lucy asked the fiddler.

"I'm crying because this crocodile is crying," replied the fiddler. "And I can't make him stop."

"And neither can I," said the clown.

"And neither can I," said Mrs Mumbles.

"Boo hoo hoo!" cried the crocodile.

"Quack quack!" said the ducks, who were getting hungry by now. So Lucy said,

"Why are you crying, Mr Crocodile?"

"I'm crying because there's something up there," he said. "In that tree."

"What is it?" asked Mrs Mumbles and the clown and the fiddler and Lucy and her mother.

"W - e- l - l," said the crocodile. "It's *big* and *hairy* and *scary* . . ."

"O - o - o - o - h!" said Mrs Mumbles and the clown and the fiddler and Lucy and her mother, trembling with fear.

"And I think it's going to jump down on us - any - minute - N - O - W!" cried the crocodile.

Just then a great big huge enormous spider jumped out of the tree.

"Aaaaagh!" cried Mrs Mumbles.

"Aaaaagh!" cried the clown.

"Aaaaagh!" cried the fiddler.

"Aaaaagh!" cried Lucy and her mother.

"Quack!" cried the ducks.

Then they all leapt up from the bench and ran out of the park; and the crocodile ran after them.

Mrs Mumbles took them all home to her house where she gave them lemonade and biscuits to make them feel better after their terrible fright. They spent a jolly afternoon dancing to the fiddler's music and laughing with the clown. At tea time they all went home, and that might seem like the end of the story.

But it isn't . . .

The next day, Mrs Mumbles set off as usual to feed the ducks at the park. When she got there she found somebody was already sitting on her favourite bench, under her favourite tree . . .

It was a gigantic gorilla.

And the gigantic gorilla was crying great big huge enormous gorilla tears . . .

WOOF'S
WORST DAY

Patricia Cleveland-Peck

The String family lived in Mrs Bun's kitchen. Lots of String people do that – live secretly in our houses. You've probably passed quite a few of them without noticing, because they are very small, only about the size of a pencil, and when they hear humans coming they unknot themselves so they look just like bits of string. They like to be useful, and spend a lot of time tying things up and holding things together for humans.

One rainy day the String children were bored and cross, and Mrs String was tired of having them under her feet. Worst of all was Woof, the long-haired stringhound. He kept trotting outside to see if it had stopped raining. When he came in wet and muddy and shook himself for the umpteenth time, Mrs String lost her temper. She had just cleaned the floor and she told him to decide once and for all whether he wanted to stay in or get out. Woof took one look at her furious face and slunk out.

On this particular day, Mrs Bun was feeling fed up too. It was too rainy to go in the garden, which was what she really wanted to do, so she decided to make a cherry cake to cheer herself up.

Then she got the vacuum cleaner out and had just made a start on cleaning the house when the doorbell rang. It was a friend of hers, so she made a pot of tea and they sat down together eating the cake.

Late that night when the wind was whistling round the house and Mrs Bun had gone to bed, Mr String called Woof for his last walk. Woof, however, was not in his basket.

"That's funny," said Mr String. "It's not like old Woof to stay out in the cold."

"You'd better have a look for him, Sisal dear," said Mrs String, feeling sorry she had been cross. "The poor old dog." But the kitchen clock had struck eleven before Mr String returned, his face wet and worried.

"Not a sign of him," he said. "I called and whistled – but nothing."

The String children, who had all woken up when they heard what had happened, looked at him with gloomy faces.

"Now tell me," he said, taking off his raincoat, "who saw him last?"

"He was here this afternoon," said Hemp, thinking hard. "Yes, I remember after Mrs Bun had her tea, I saw him go and snuffle about for crumbs."

"So did Twine," said Flax, the little String girl. "He gorged himself."

"You didn't, did you, Twine?" asked Mrs String in an angry voice. "You know how cross that makes me. Any crumbs we collect from Mrs Bun are to be brought home and eaten at table like good children."

"Tell-tale tit," said Twine, giving Flax a furious punch. "Tittle-tattle . . ."

"Rooting around just like a pig, he was," added Flax, dodging his blows.

"Stop that, children," said Mr String. "Quarrelling won't help find that dog. Now Twine, did you see Woof afterwards?"

"No, I just got a few crumbs off the table while he got some off the floor. I mean, what harm . . ." He caught his father's eye. "No, I thought he came back here after me."

"I remember," said Flax thoughtfully. "After she had tea, when her friend went home Mrs Bun gave the floor a quick clean with the snake-box machine."

"What snake-box machine?" asked Hemp.

"That noisy thing with a box one end and a long sort of snake tube she walks about with."

"Oh, you mean the vacuum cleaner," said Hemp, laughing at his sister. "Snake-box, ha, ha, ha."

"Oh my goodness," said Mr String, going white. "The vacuum must have got him! How many times have I told you children to keep away from dangerous things like that?"

"The vacuum's eaten Woof," said Twine. "Gobbled him up . . ." He began to cry.

"We'll probably never see him again," said Flax.

"Do you think he's dead?" asked Hemp.

"Now," said Mr String, "let's think about it sensibly. The vacuum thing just sucks up the dust and dirt into a big bag inside it. It doesn't eat the dirt; it's not alive. When the bag is full, Mrs Bun empties it. The thing is, has she emptied it since Woof got sucked in, and if so where?"

93

"I know where," said Hemp. "She always empties it in the garden, on the compost heap. I remember last summer when I was tying up outdoor tomatoes I saw her do that and thought how funny humans are. First they scatter rubbish all over their houses and then they collect it carefully in these special machines and empty it into their gardens."

"But I don't think she did empty it today," Flax interrupted. "She just put it away and then went and watched television in the evening."

"So," said Mr String, "as far as we know Woof may still be in there. We'll just have to organize a rescue party. Where does she keep the vacuum cleaner?"

"In the cupboard under the stairs."

"I'm scared," whispered Flax, knotting her hand tightly into Twine's. "Are you sure the vacuum thing won't eat us?"

They were standing in the hall. It was dark except for a faint moonbeam which shone eerily through the glass in the front door. The only sound was the ticking of the grandfather clock in the corner.

"Of course not, come on." Mr String untied himself and slipped under the cupboard door. The others followed him. Inside it was even darker and there was a strong smell of floor polish.

"I can't see a thing," grumbled Hemp.

"Wait a minute." Mr String brought out the luminous dial of an old wristwatch which he used as a torch. "That's better." They looked around.

"There it is," said Mrs String. The vacuum cleaner lay in two parts. The long hose was coiled round a hook and the box part stood on its end.

"Listen, I can hear something," whispered Hemp. A muffled scrabbling sound, faint and far off.

"It might be mice," shuddered Mrs String. (No String likes the thought of a mouse's sharp teeth . . .)

"It might be Woof, though," said Mr String. He went up to the machine and called, as loudly as he dared, "Woof, can you hear me?"

The noise came again, unmistakably louder. It just could have been barking . . .

They all strained their ears and then Mr String climbed up on top of the vacuum cleaner and looked down the hole where the hose fitted.

"I can see a movement, right down at the bottom in all the dust. But the sides are smooth; there's nothing for it, we'll have to form a chain and lift him out. All join end to end and lower me down."

Silently the String family obeyed.

"I'll knot him to me and when I say so, you pull us up. No letting go now, I don't want to end up down there too." Mr String disappeared into the dark cavern of the cleaner bag and the rest of the family held on as tightly as they could.

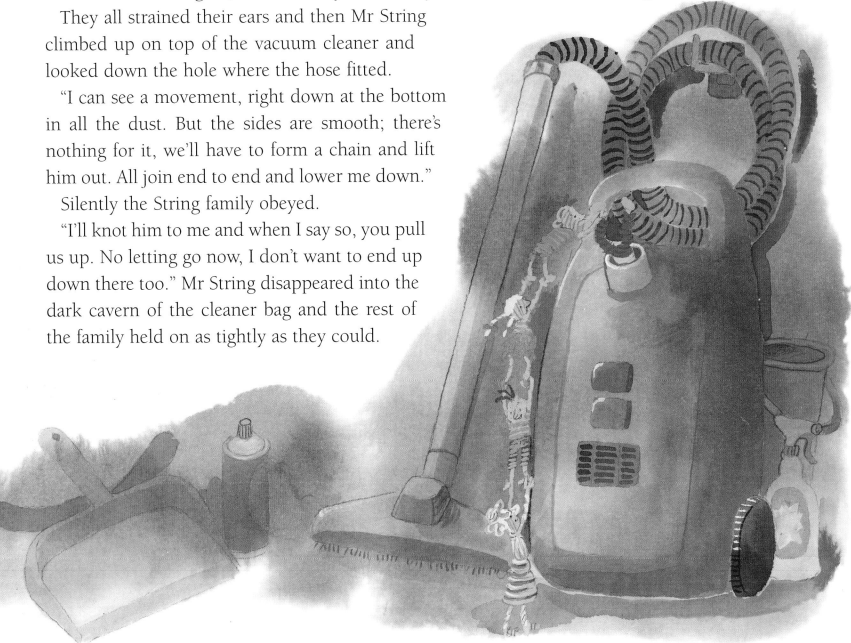

From below came a series of confused sounds followed by a big cloud of dust. Then the faint command, "Pull away!"

They all tugged and tugged until Mr String's head, dusty as a coal miner's, appeared at the opening.

"Look who I've got," he said, scrambling out. Woof, thickly covered with filthy dust, began to bark and wag his tail so vigorously that within a minute the whole family were as dirty as he was. Their dusty faces full of smiles, the children hugged Woof, Mrs String hugged Mr String and Mr String hugged the whole family.

Back home, Mr String fetched thimble-buckets of warm water and Mrs String prepared baths for them all. Even Woof was given a good scrub.

"To think only this morning I was worrying about a few muddy paw marks," said Mrs String. "You certainly got your own back on me, Woof, you silly old dog." But Woof, tired out from his bath and his adventures, had already fallen fast asleep.

THE TINDERBOX

Hans Christian Andersen

retold by *Lucy Coats*

One summer's day, in a land so far away it is not on any map, a soldier called Hans came marching down a little winding country lane.

"*Tan-ta-ta-ra-ta-ree!*" he sang as he marched, and the brass buttons on his beautiful red uniform shone in the sunshine, and dazzled the birds into silence. As he came round a bend, Hans saw an ugly old witch standing in his path, so he stopped and stood to attention. *Snick* went his heels, and *snack* went his hand as he saluted.

"Oh!" said the witch. "What a splendid young man you are. Would you like me to make your fortune?"

Well, Hans needed a fortune badly, there were no wars to fight at that time and he was very poor, but he was also a cautious man, so he said, "Why me, grandmother?"

The witch smiled a smile that showed all her black and broken teeth, and replied, "I like soldiers, and besides, I need a strong young man to help me.

My grandmother left her old tinderbox down that hollow tree, and I'm too old to climb down there myself and get it."

Then she beckoned him even closer and whispered in his ear.

"Beware! The tree is guarded, but if you do exactly as I say all will be well. Now listen carefully! Inside the tree are three treasure rooms. The first is guarded by a red dog with eyes as big as dinner plates. The second is guarded by a white dog with eyes as big as cartwheels. The third is guarded by a blue dog with eyes as big as moons. If you take my apron with you and place each dog on it as you enter its room, they will not harm you. You may help yourself to the treasure, and all I ask is that you bring back the tinderbox from the third room."

Hans agreed, and soon the old witch was lowering him down into the tree on a strong rope.

As he reached the bottom, hundreds of lamps burst into flame, and he at once saw the entrance to the first room. Clutching the witch's apron, he went in. There, sitting on a large chest, exactly as the witch had said, was a red dog with eyes as big as dinner plates.

"Hum," said Hans as the dog started to growl at him. But he was a brave man (he wouldn't have been a soldier otherwise) and so he went up to it and lifted it onto the witch's apron, when it immediately became quiet and wagged its tail. He opened the chest, which was full to the brim with copper coins. Hans quickly filled his pockets, and went on to the next room.

There sat an even bigger white dog with eyes as big as cartwheels. It bared its teeth at Hans, but, like the first dog, was quieted by sitting on the apron. The second chest was full of silver, so Hans emptied his pockets of copper and filled them again with silver, and his rucksack too.

Then he went on to the third room.

The blue dog with eyes as big as moons was simply enormous and its huge eyes lit up the room like a thousand candles. Hans quickly lifted it onto the apron and flung open the chest. It was full of gold, so he emptied all his silver out and stuffed as much gold as he could into his pockets, his rucksack, his shoes, his hat – everywhere! Then he started to leave.

"Have you remembered my tinderbox?" screeched a voice from above. Hans had not remembered, but he soon found the box and put it safely inside his coat. Past the dogs and up the rope he went till he was out in the sunshine again.

"Where's my tinderbox?" screamed the witch. "Give it to me now or I'll turn you into a toad!"

Hans didn't like being talked to like that, after all his bravery with the dogs, so he picked the witch up, and dropped her down the tree. Then he marched rather quickly down the road until her screeches of anger faded into the distance.

Later that day, he reached a city. It was market day, and the streets were bustling with farmers and their wives, and their animals and carts. Hans pushed his way through the crowds and sniffed at the good smells of cooking and baking until he found his way to a nice old inn. He soon found a room to stay in and some fine new clothes to spend his gold on. As he looked out of the inn window, he saw a large copper tower rising above the rooftops.

"Tell me," he said to the innkeeper, "what is that?"

"Oh, that," said the innkeeper. "That's the tower where the Princess Celia is locked up. Her fairy godmother said she'd marry a poor soldier, and so her father, King Blodgrad, is keeping her shut up there till he's got her married off to a nice rich prince instead."

Hans was very interested in the princess, but he soon forgot about her in the excitement of spending his money. He spent it on horses and carriages, on gambling and jewels, and on his new friends. Soon he had spent it all, and he had nothing left except his pipe, his uniform, and the witch's tinderbox, still safely tucked inside his coat pocket. Hans took it out for the first time and looked at it.

"It's a bit battered," he said to himself. "I wonder if it still works." He sighed as he filled his pipe with the last scrap of tobacco. *Scritch* went the tinderbox as Hans lit the pipe, and *bump* – there was the red dog with eyes as big as dinner plates, sitting right in front of him.

"Master!" growled the dog. "Command me!" So Hans commanded him to fetch some money from the hollow tree.

As soon as he had rented a comfortable room, Hans scratched the tinderbox again. *Scritch, scritch*, and there was the white dog with eyes as big as cartwheels. *Scritch, scritch, scritch* and the blue dog with eyes as big as moons appeared.

"Master," they growled. "Command us!"

Hans was bored with jewels and clothes and his new friends had disappeared when his money did. So he looked out of his window and thought and thought. As he did so, he remembered Princess Celia, shut up and lonely in her copper tower, and he commanded the dogs to go and fetch her. The dogs soon appeared again, carrying the princess fast asleep on their backs. She was so beautiful that Hans bent down and kissed her. She smiled in her sleep, and then the dogs took her back again.

Next morning the princess was telling everyone about a strange dream she'd had about being stolen away by two dogs with huge eyes (she didn't tell about the kiss!). King Blodgrad was worried, and set her waiting woman to watch through the night. Sure enough the dogs appeared again, and the waiting woman ran through the streets after them and marked a white cross on the soldier's door. But the dog with eyes as big as moons noticed the mark, and he quickly made crosses on every door in town, so that Hans should not be caught.

The king was furious, and so the next night Queen Ethelrida (who was a very clever lady) put a little sack of grain in her daughter's pocket, and made a hole so it would trickle out if she was moved. As they carried the princess through the town, neither of the dogs noticed the little trail of grain leading right into Hans's room.

I like stories with magic in them!

The next morning the guards burst through the door and dragged him off to prison. Hans didn't like prison much, and he liked it even less the next morning when the guards came again and dragged him before the king, the queen, the princess and all the court.

"Wretched fellow," roared the king. "Have you any last request before I kill you for stealing my daughter?"

Hans nodded bravely. "I should like to light a last pipe with my old tinderbox, please, Your Majesty." So the tinderbox was fetched, and Hans lit his pipe. *Scritch scritch scritch! Bump bump bump!* There were the three huge dogs, each carrying a mountain of treasure which they laid at the king's feet.

"Ha!" said King Blodgrad. "You must be a prince! Only a prince could have so much treasure. Perhaps I'd better not kill you after all." And he took Princess Celia's hand and gave it to Hans, who kissed her as she smiled at him happily and snuggled under his elbow.

And so it came about that the fairy godmother was right (as they usually are), and the poor soldier married his princess. Their wedding was a most splendid and joyful affair, and at their wedding feast the three dogs sat in the place of honour and stared and stared and stared at all the guests with their three pairs of enormous eyes. The copper tower was torn down soon after, and Prince Hans and Princess Celia lived happily for the rest of their lives.

THE MAGIC SCISSORS

Loes Spaander

Once upon a time, far, far away in a half forgotten part of the world, between high mountains and a deep blue lake, there was a little Chinese boy and his name was Liu Chu.

He lived with his father and mother in a little bamboo hut and he was very happy. All day long he played in the sand or he sat in the sun and looked at the birds and the flowers. And when he was hungry his mother gave him a bowl of rice, and he ate it with his fingers, and nobody minded.

One day his mother said to him, "Liu Chu, there is not enough rice today. Go to the lake and catch some fish for dinner."

Liu Chu, who was a good little boy, went to the back of the hut to fetch his fishing net. Then he trotted off to the lake.

It was a long way and the day was very hot. But Liu Chu was used to the sun and did not mind a bit. He whistled as he went and soon reached the lake. There he threw his net into the water and caught a beautiful big red-and-blue-and-silver fish. Liu Chu was very glad, but the red-and-blue-and-silver fish said, "Dear Liu Chu, please, please let me go and I promise you a wonderful pair of magic scissors; whatever you cut with them will come to life."

So Liu Chu let the red-and-blue-and-silver fish go and found himself holding a wonderful pair of scissors instead.

Liu Chu was delighted. He took a scrap of golden paper and cut out a beautiful little castle. No sooner was it ready than it grew and grew, and to his surprise the boy saw an immense golden castle arising before him.

Then Liu Chu thought of the lovely garden that should surround it, and with the scissors he cut out tree after tree, flower after flower, the one more beautiful than the other, and they all grew and became real. And he also cut out pretty little birds, that filled the air with their sweet music.

Liu Chu then ran home to fetch his parents. But when he saw them in their ragged old clothes, he decided to make them new ones first.

He set to work with his scissors, and the little paper garments he made became magnificent clothes of silk and brocade.

Soon they were all dressed in them and Liu Chu led the way to the castle. His parents were full of admiration and wonder and went to look inside. Liu Chu, left alone in the garden, decided to make himself some playmates. He cut some paper dolls. They fluttered around him and became lifelike, and in no time a whole swarm of cheerful little boys and girls were dancing around him, crying happily, "Liu Chu, be our friend, come and play with us."

Thus Liu Chu made everything under the sun that should fill a little boy with happiness. The castle became their new home. There were so many rooms that nobody had ever seen them all, and each one was furnished in grand style and with exquisite taste. There were the most precious toys and delightful books, but yet, the more he had the unhappier he became. One by one his old pleasures were taken away from him.

If he ate with his fingers his father would box his ears and say, "What are your chopsticks for, young rascal?"

And if he played in the sand, his mother would scold and say, "Liu Chu dear, think of your beautiful new clothes, you'll spoil them."

Worst of all, there was no more time to play. All day long from breakfast to suppertime there were lessons to study. Learned professors came to teach Liu Chu reading and writing and arithmetic, geography, history and oh! so many other things. Liu Chu was sure he never would remember all he had to learn.

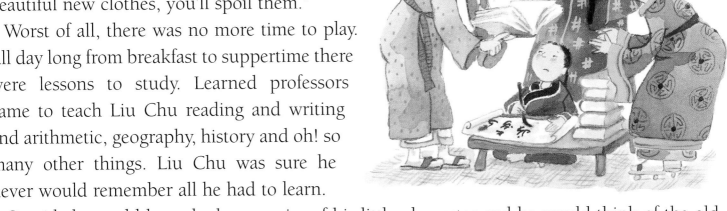

Outside he could hear the happy cries of his little playmates and he would think of the old days, when he, too, was out in the sun, laughing and playing, watching the birds and the flowers.

So, day by day, little Liu Chu grew less happy. One night he could not sleep, but lay tossing about in his bed. At last he got up and softly went out of his bedroom.

He tiptoed through the sleeping palace and silent gardens and ventured out of the gate.

The moon was shining very brightly, making a magic world out of the one Liu Chu knew so well. He shivered a little with the cold of the night, but he went on bravely to find his way to the lake. There he looked for his friend, the red-and-blue-and-silver fish.

"Fish," he cried, "red-and-blue-and-silver fish, it's me, Liu Chu. I am no longer happy. Can't you help me?"

The fish peeped out of the water. "Little friend," he said, "you have grown too rich, and wealth does not always mean happiness; take your scissors, and at sunrise whistle thrice and throw them into the lake. Then you will be rich no more, but you may be happy again."

The fish disappeared and Liu Chu sat down to wait for the sun to come up. At last, the pale dawn crept slowly over the mountains, and soon the earth was filled with light and warmth. Liu Chu threw his scissors into the lake and went home hopefully.

There he found the old bamboo hut again. His mother in her old clothes was waiting for him with a bowl of rice. She smiled at him. And Liu Chu, sitting down on the warm yellow sand to gobble up his rice, felt that once more he was the happiest boy in the world.

One Night I'm Going to Catch You!

Joy Haney

One night, Janeen woke up at midnight.

She could hear soft whispering all around her. She opened her eyes quickly . . . but she was just too late, her toys sat there pretending they'd never said a word, never, ever said a word.

Janeen said,

"One night I'm going to catch you.
I'm going to catch you with my eyes
I heard you whispering,
I know you're alive!"

Then her mummy called from downstairs, "Janeen, it's past midnight and you're still awake!"

Janeen told her, "My toys woke me up."

Her mummy said, "You should be asleep!"

The next night, at midnight, Janeen heard them talking. They had squeaky, growly, singsong voices. She opened her eyes quickly . . . but she was just too late, they sat there pretending they'd never said a word, never, ever said a word.

Janeen said,

"Next time I'm going to catch you!
I'm going to catch you with my eyes!
I heard you whispering,
I heard you talking,
I know it's you
and you're just pretending!"

Thump thump came her mummy's footsteps at the bottom of the stairs.

She called, "Janeen! I can hear you talking up there!"

Janeen said, "It wasn't me!"

Her mummy said, "Go to sleep!"

The next night, at midnight, Janeen was waiting but she fell asleep just as her toys started giggling. She opened her eyes quickly . . . but she was just too late, they sat there pretending they'd never giggled, never, ever giggled.

Janeen said,

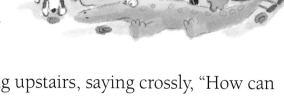

"Ooooh, I'm going to catch you!
I'm going to catch you with my eyes!
I heard you whispering,
I heard you talking,
I heard you giggling . . .
I'll catch you next time!!"

Thump thump thump came her mummy leaping upstairs, saying crossly, "How can one small girl make so much NOISE!"

Janeen cried, "It was my toys!"

Her mummy said, "One more sound and I'll be really annoyed!"

The next night, at midnight, Janeen thought she was dreaming and in the dream lots of funny voices were singing. Then she knew it was those toys. She opened her eyes quickly . . . but she was just too late, they sat there pretending they'd never sung a song, never, ever sung a song.

Janeen said,

"One night I really will catch you!
I'm going to catch you with my eyes!
I heard you whispering,
I heard you talking,
I heard you giggling,
I heard you singing!
I'll catch you next time!"

Thump thump THUMP came her mummy, running upstairs, shouting, "What a racket! It gets worse and worse!"

"My toys WERE SINGING!" yelled Janeen.

Her mummy yelled, "Be quiet! And please go to sleep!"

The next night, at midnight, Janeen was awake but she pretended, very cleverly, to be fast asleep. She snored loudly, and when those toys began to laugh she opened her eyes quickly . . . and *she wasn't too late!* She cried, "AH HA! I CAN SEE YOU! I'VE CAUGHT YOU WITH MY EYES!" The toys looked surprised. Then they all fell about laughing and wanted to play. Janeen said, "Let's play bouncing on the bed! Can you bounce this high? Or this high?" They bounced higher and higher and giggled and laughed louder and louder!

THUMP THUMP THUMP came Janeen's mummy dashing upstairs, shouting, "I CANNOT BELIEVE MY EARS! HOW CAN ONE SMALL GIRL SOUND LIKE A WILD PARTY? LIKE A CHIMPANZEE ON A TRAMPOLINE! LIKE A PARROT SINGING IN THE BATH! ENOUGH IS ENOUGH!" And she threw open Janeen's door . . . but she was just too late, Janeen and the toys just lay there pretending they'd never been bouncing or laughing or giggling, never been talking or even been whispering. Never, ever.

One night, at midnight, Janeen had a nightmare and she called out for her mummy to make her feel better. Her mummy said, "Oooh, poor Janeen, I'll stay here beside you while you go back to sleep."

She put all her toys around her like a nest, teddy by her feet and monkey by her head, and all the others tucked in by her arms and legs.

Then she said, "Sleep well, Janeen."

And when she had gone the toys whispered, "Sweet dreams."

How the Rabbit Got His Hop

Michael Lawrence

Now you may think that the rabbit always hopped. Not so. Oh no. Once upon a time the rabbit walked everywhere, though sometimes he broke into a run when he was in a hurry. It never occurred to him that there might be some other way for him to get about.

Until the day of the Great Storm, that is.

Rabbit missed most of the storm because he was away visiting his old friend Weasel that day, and he had no idea how bad it had been till he trotted homeward with a spring in his step and a whistle in his teeth, thinking how very good it was to be alive.

But then he saw the great tree that had fallen across the road home and the great boulders that had tumbled down the hill, blocking the valley on either side, and he stopped in his tracks, thinking that maybe it wasn't such a good day after all.

Well of course Rabbit tried to climb over the tree that had fallen across the road, but the tree was much too high and broad for someone as small as he, who could only walk and run anyway.

116

"Make way!" cried a voice.

Rabbit made way, and Wallaby bounded past, and over, and off into the distance.

"It's all right for you!" Rabbit shouted after him.

"Watch out, Rabbit!" cried another voice.

Rabbit watched out, and Goat skipped and skedaddled over and on, hind legs kicking.

"Show-off!" yelled Rabbit.

Next, Hare came by and skippety-skipped over the obstacles, and then Grasshopper hippety-hopped over, and Frog froggety-frogged over, all as easy as winking.

"What about *me*?" wailed Rabbit, who couldn't for the life of him get over, however hard he tried.

"Better get a move on, Rabbit," said Wolf as he jumped over. "Storm's coming back."

"Don't dilly-dally," said Mouse, who scrambled over without any trouble at all. "Lightning's on the way."

"Daft to stand round here," said Crow as he spread his wings and flew over. "Thunder clouds a'rolling."

And back came the storm that Rabbit had been lucky enough to miss earlier. First came the clouds, great black scowling clouds rolling across the roof of the world, and drip, drip, dripping over Rabbit as they passed. Then, as the rain fell harder, in great galloping gallumphing squishes, the lightning shivered across the sky and struck the earth all hard and brittle.

"Oo-hoo-hoo," said Rabbit, who didn't care for lightning one bit.

The thunder came last of all, but what thunder it was! Out of the black scowling clouds it came, like the breakfast bellow of an ill-tempered giant, such a terrible, shaky-quaky roar that the earth shook and quivered and covered its head and sobbed into its handkerchief.

Rabbit's ears stood up like two telegraph poles either side of a wet road, and when his ears went up the rest of him followed, sharp and sudden, as though a rocket had been set off under him. So high did Rabbit's fright jump him that he thought he would never come down, but he did come down, and when he looked about him he found, to his great surprise, that he stood on the other side of the fallen tree.

"How did I get here?" he wondered, straightening out his dripping whiskers and setting his sopping ears to rights.

But before he could work it out, the lightning shivered again, and struck the ground again, and this time it danced around his feet as if to snag his rabbity toes. Well, naturally, Rabbit jumped aside, and then he jumped aside again, but still the lightning tried to snag his toes, so he kicked up his heels and off he went, helter-skelter, for all he was worth, leaping and jumping all the way to his doorstep, where he stood all out of breath and dizzy, but glad as glad can be to have got there so fast and easy.

Rabbit never walked again from that day forth, or even ran quite the way he used to. He'd forgotten how.

"Oh, how I wish," he was heard to grumble as the years hopped by, "how I wish I could go for a walk once in a while. You can't beat a nice quiet little walk when the mood's upon you . . ."

I don't know. Some rabbits are never satisfied.

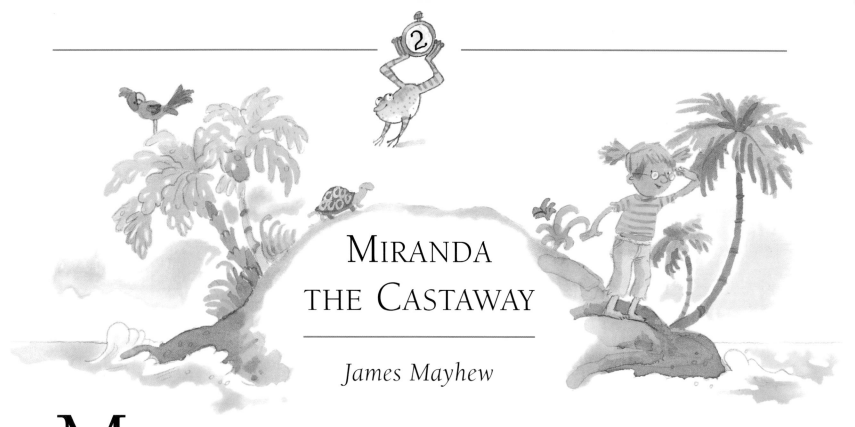

MIRANDA THE CASTAWAY

James Mayhew

Miranda was shipwrecked. She was cast away on a desert island, all by herself. She waited to be rescued, but no one came.

Miranda didn't know what she was supposed to do.

The sharks knew what to do. Miranda watched them eat fish. She watched the turtles eat seaweed, and the birds eat fruit and drink nectar, and the snakes eat birds, and the monkeys eat nuts. She saw that even the spiders knew what to eat.

She wanted some food and water, but seawater was too salty and the pools were full of insects. At last she found a spring with clean fresh water and she drank some. Then she took the braces off her teeth, tied them to a shoelace and caught a fish. She couldn't bear to eat it, so she threw it back into the sea.

Then Miranda wondered if there was any fruit she could eat. She struggled through the trees and recognised mangoes and starfruit, bananas and nuts. She ate lots of them.

By now Miranda was tired and wanted to go to sleep. The sharks rested in the water. The turtles had laid their eggs on the sand. The birds had their nests, the snakes and spiders their holes, the monkeys their trees. Miranda tried to sleep on the beach under the stars, but it was cold, and the sounds of the sea and the island kept her awake.

So the next morning, Miranda decided to build a house of her own. She thought she would be safest in a tree. She put logs between the branches for the floor, gathered leaves and wove them together with creepers to make the walls, and filled the gaps with mud. She magnified the sun with her glasses and started a fire. It would keep her warm at night and be useful for cooking.

It was hard work fetching water, so she hollowed out bamboo sticks to make giant straws that ran all the way from the spring to the treehouse.

Every day Miranda found new things to use on the island. She used shells to eat off and coconuts to drink from. She pulled threads from the vines to use as string and made necklaces with stones and shells and a sunhat out of leaves. She planted seeds and grew flowers and vegetables in her garden.

121

Miranda built more and more. She built a bedroom, a kitchen, a bathroom, even a toilet.

Miranda was having fun on the island. No school, no bedtime, definitely no bath and hairwash night. It seemed she had everything she could possibly need.

One day she saw a ship, and she waved and shouted. But nobody saw her because she was so small. Although she waited for the ship to come back, it never did.

Miranda felt lonely. The sharks had each other. The turtles had a big family. So did the monkeys and all the other animals. Even the spiders had a family. She tried to make friends with them, but it wasn't the same.

So Miranda built a raft to sail away on. She was sad to leave her garden and her treehouse, but she didn't belong on the island. Miranda wanted her family, and it was time to go home.

I think Miranda liked her desert island. Would you?

FELIX AND
THE DRAGON

Angela McAllister

Felix was Prince of the Castle, Prince of the Mountains and Prince of the Forest. He had one thousand precious things but he kept them all to himself.

Every day he wandered alone in the forest with only his shadow to play beside him.

One morning Felix saw a white shining among the leaves, as if the moon had dropped into the trees. When he crept close he found a dragon curled up asleep in the mouth of a cave.

"Wake up, White Dragon," Felix commanded. "This is my cave in my forest. You cannot sleep here."

The White Dragon opened his eyes and stretched out his great wings. "I must guard this cave," he said, "because it holds my treasure, which is the most wonderful in the land."

"It cannot be as wonderful as my treasure," boasted Felix. "I have a golden horn that can call all the beasts of the forest and the birds of the sky."

"So have I," said the dragon. And he fetched a golden horn from deep inside his cave.

When the dragon blew the horn a great galloping was heard and all the beasts of the forest gathered around, and the treetops were filled with singing birds.

Felix the Prince rode on the back of a red stag and then he climbed to the top of the peacock tree. And the White Dragon danced with the unicorn.

"I have even more wonderful things," the dragon cried. "I have a flag of rainbow silk that will stir up the four winds."

"So have I," said Felix. And he went home to his deep cellar and returned with a shimmering silk flag.

When Felix the Prince waved the flag above his head, four breezes blew across the forest floor. Then, with one great gust, they lifted him up into the air, over the treetops, towards the mountains. The White Dragon opened his wings and flew beside Felix. Together they swooped and soared among the ice forests.

When it was time to return, the dragon let Felix ride upon his back. "I have treasures even more wonderful," laughed Felix the Prince with the wind in his hair. "I have a casket of powder that will fill the sky with fireworks."

"So have I," said the dragon, and he disappeared into his deep cave. When he returned with a silver casket he flew in low circles above Felix, sprinkling powder upon the grass.

Suddenly the sky grew dark and fireworks sprouted from the earth, shot high through the trees and exploded into stars. Felix the Prince conducted the fireworks like a grand orchestra and the White Dragon breathed, spinning fireballs high into the sky. But slowly the fireworks died and the blue sky returned.

"Now which one of us has the most wonderful treasure?" asked the White Dragon as Felix the Prince shook the sparkles from his hair.

"Let us both bring one more treasure," said Felix, "and then we shall see."

So the dragon set off down the long winding chambers of his cave and Felix rode back to his castle. The castle cellar was deep underground and Felix counted five hundred steps as he climbed down to his treasure house.

Meanwhile the dragon went deeper and deeper into his cave until he reached the entrance to his treasure chamber. Just as he rolled back the heavy rock to climb inside, Felix unbolted the great oak door of his cellar, and . . . there they were, Felix and the dragon, face to face.

"This is my treasure!" cried Felix the Prince.

"But this is my treasure!" cried the White Dragon.

The castle cellar and the dragon's cave were the very same place. They had been sharing the same treasure all along.

"So we both have the most wonderful treasure in the land!" exclaimed the dragon. And Felix laughed.

"We both have a thousand precious things."

From that day Felix, Prince of the Castle, Prince of the Mountains, Prince of the Forest shared the most wonderful treasure with the White Dragon. And he never had to play with his shadow again.

THE TWO GIANTS

Michael Foreman

Once, long ago, two giants lived in a beautiful country. In summer it was warm, and in winter the land was even more beautiful under snow.

Each day the giants walked together among the mountains and through the forests, taking care not to step on the trees. Birds made nests in their beards, and everywhere the giants went thrushes and nightingales sang.

One day while paddling in the sea, the two giants found a pink shell. The shell was very bright and both giants admired it.

"It will look lovely on a string round my neck," said the giant called Boris.

"Oh no! It will be on a string round *my* neck," said Sam, the other giant, "and it will look better there."

For the first time in their lives they began to argue. And as they did the sun went behind a cloud and the cloud became bigger and blacker. The wind blew and blew and the waves and clouds grew and grew. It began to rain. The more the giants argued, the colder the day became. The waves swept higher and higher up the beach.

Boris and Sam began hurriedly pulling on their socks. Before they could put their shoes on, a huge wave completely covered the beach.

The wave swept away the shoes and the shell.

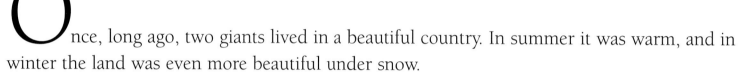

128

The giants were furious and threw stones at each other as they ran towards the mountains to escape the flood. Soon the whole country was covered by water except for the tops of two mountains, which became the only islands in a wide, cold sea. Boris lived in one and Sam in the other.

It was cold. They liked snow, but it never snowed. Winter followed winter. The giants forgot how lovely the summers used to be. Each day was just dull and terribly cold.

They grew more angry than ever, and instead of stones they now threw huge rocks at each other. On Mondays Sam would throw a rock at Boris. On Tuesdays Boris would throw a rock at Sam. On Wednesdays it was Sam's turn to throw again, and so on, every day except Sundays, every week.

After both giants had been struck many times on the ear and nose and the tops of their heads, their anger knew no limits.

The sea was dotted with rocks which the giants had thrown, and one day Sam decided to use these rocks as giant stepping stones. He waited until Boris was asleep, then picked up his huge stone club and climbed out of his mountain. He planned to reach the other island, hit Boris on the head, and make him sleep all day and miss his turn to throw a rock.

Sam leapt onto the first rock. Then he leapt onto the second rock.

As Sam reached the third rock, Boris opened one giant eye. He saw Sam, snatched his club and, whirling it round his head, jumped out of his mountain and began leaping from rock to rock towards his enemy. The whole world shook as the two giants charged towards each other.

Suddenly both giants stopped. Sam looked at the feet of Boris. Boris looked at the feet of Sam. Each giant had one black-and-white sock and one red-and-blue sock. They stared at their odd socks for a long time.

Gradually they remembered the day the sea had covered the land. In their haste to escape the flood, the giants had got their socks mixed up. Now they could not even remember what they had been fighting about. They could only recall the years they had been friends. They dropped their clubs into the sea, and laughed and danced.

When they returned to their islands, each found a small white flower and felt the sun warm on his shoulders. The sea began to recede. Flowers grew where the water had been. The birds returned to the islands. Soon the two mountains were separated by nothing but a valley of trees. The country was large and beautiful once more.

Sam and Boris sat among the flowers, and sometimes a grasshopper would jump onto Sam's ear, or a butterfly would land on Boris's nose and birds would sit on the tops of their heads amidst the hair and flowers. The giants were happy. The seasons came and went as before. Sometimes the giants strode about their country, deep with grass or leaves or snow. Sometimes they made giant footprints in the sand by the sea. Sometimes they just lay in the woods which were full of birds and marigolds.

Whatever they did, they always wore odd socks. Even when one of them had a new pair, he always gave one sock to the other giant – just in case!

THE THREE LITTLE PIGS AND THE BIG BAD WOLF

Vivian French

Once upon a time there were three little pigs and they lived with their mother in a rather small sty.

"Oink! Oink!" said their mother one fine bright morning. "Dear little pigs, I have something to say to you."

"What is it, Mother?" asked the three little pigs.

"Oink," said Mother Pig, and a tear trickled down her snout. "This sty is too small for the four of us. You are big little pigs now, and you must go out into the wide world and find houses of your own."

"Hurrah!" shouted the first little pig.

"What fun!" said the second little pig.

"Goodness me!" said the third little pig.

"Oink," said Mother Pig. "It's a fine bright day, so you'd better go at once." She sniffed. "Do be careful."

133

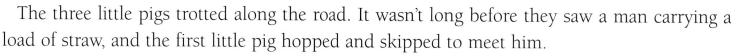

The three little pigs scurried around and packed their bags.

"Cheerio, Mother!" they called. "We'll see you soon!"

"OINK!" said their mother, and she waved them goodbye.

The three little pigs trotted along the road. It wasn't long before they saw a man carrying a load of straw, and the first little pig hopped and skipped to meet him.

"Please may I have some straw for my house?" he asked. "I'm going to build a house for my very very own!"

"I'll be glad to give you some straw," said the man. "But you look out for the Big Bad Wolf!"

"Pooh!" said the first little pig. "I don't care a fig for the Big Bad Wolf!" And he took his straw and built himself an untidy little house by the side of the road.

"Goodbye, brother! Goodbye, sister!" he said, and he hopped and skipped into his little straw house and went to sleep.

The two little pigs trotted along the road. It wasn't long before they saw a man carrying a load of sticks, and the second little pig hurried along to meet him.

"Please may I have some sticks for my house?" he asked. "I'm going to build a house for my very very own!"

"I'll be glad to give you some sticks," said the man. "But you look out for the Big Bad Wolf!"

"No worries," said the second little pig. "That Big Bad Wolf won't come bothering me!" And he took his sticks and built himself a rough little house by the side of the road.

"Goodbye, sister!" he said, and he hurried into his little stick house and went to sleep.

The third little pig trotted along the road. It wasn't long before she saw a man carrying a load of bricks, and the third little pig trotted along to meet him.

"Please may I have some bricks for my house?" she asked. "I'm going to build a house for my very very own."

"I'll be glad to give you some bricks," said the man. "But you look out for the big bad wolf!"

"I certainly will," said the third little pig. "And thank you for your kindness." And she took her bricks and built herself a neat little house. It took her a long time, but at last it was finished.

"Phew!" sighed the third little pig, and she trotted into her little brick house. She was very tired, but she piled up a heap of sticks by the fire and filled a large pan with water.

"You never know who may come to call," she said to herself, "and hot water always comes in handy." And the third little pig tucked herself up and went to sleep.

At the other end of the road the Big Bad Wolf was leaning on Mother Pig's sty.

"No little pigs, I see," he said. "Got too big, did they?"

"Indeed they did," said Mother Pig proudly. "Off they went, as good as gold."

"Well, well, well," said the Big Bad Wolf. "Went down the road this way, did they?"

"Oink," said Mother Pig.

"Fancy that," said the Big Bad Wolf. "I'm going that way myself, as it happens. I'll give them your love if I see them."

The Big Bad Wolf hurried down the road. It wasn't long before he came to the untidy little house of straw, and he smiled a toothy smile.

"Little pig!" he called. "Will you come out and play?"

"Pooh!" shouted the first little pig. "Go away, you horrid old wolf!"

"Aha!" said the Big Bad Wolf. "Then I'll huff, and I'll puff, and I'll BLOW your house down!"

136

And he huffed and he puffed and he BLEW the house down.

The first little pig ran and ran, and the Big Bad Wolf ran after him . . . but the first little pig ran faster. He dashed into his brother's rough little house of sticks.

"Help!" he puffed. "The Big Bad Wolf is coming!"

The Big Bad Wolf hurried down the road after the first little pig. It wasn't long before he came to the rough little house of sticks, and he smiled a very toothy smile.

"Little pig!" he called, "Will you come out to play?"

"Go away!" shouted the second little pig. "And don't come bothering me!"

"Aha!" said the Big Bad Wolf. "Then I'll huff, and I'll puff, and I'll BLOW your house down!"

And he huffed and he puffed and he huffed and he puffed and he BLEW the house down.

The two little pigs ran and ran and ran, and the Big Bad Wolf ran after them . . . but the two little pigs ran faster.

They dashed into their sister's neat little house of bricks.

"Help!" they panted. "The Big Bad Wolf is coming!"

"He is, is he?" said the third little pig, and she lit her fire and put the pan of water on to boil . . . just below the chimney.

The Big Bad Wolf hurried down the road after the two little pigs. It wasn't long before he came to the neat little house of bricks, and he smiled a very *very* toothy smile.

"Little pig!" he called. "Will you come out to play?"

"Certainly not!" shouted the third little pig.

"Aha!" said the Big Bad Wolf. "Then I'll huff, and I'll puff, and I'll BLOW your house down!"

And he huffed and he puffed and he huffed and he puffed and he HUFFED and he PUFFED . . . but he couldn't blow the brick house down.

"Ho ho!" said the Big Bad Wolf. "There's more than one way to catch a pig!" And he scrambled up onto the roof of the little brick house and squeezed himself into the chimney.

Scrabble scrabble scrabble! The Big Bad Wolf slipped and slid down and down.

"Yum yum yum!" said the Big Bad Wolf to himself. "Nearly time for–"

Splashhhhhh!

The Big Bad Wolf landed in the bubbling boiling water.

Yaroooooo!!

The Big Bad Wolf leapt out. He howled and he yowled and he shrieked and he yelled and he rushed out of the door and down the road and over the hill . . . and he never ever *ever* bothered the three little pigs again.

THE RARE SPOTTED BIRTHDAY PARTY

Margaret Mahy

It was Mark's birthday in two days' time but he was not happy about it.

His mother had made a wonderful cake, round, brown and full of nuts and raisins and cherries. There were balloons and party hats hidden in the high cupboard with the Christmas decorations and old picture books. But Mark was not happy.

It was his birthday in two days' time and he had the measles.

Everyone was getting the measles.

"Measles are going around," said Mark's little sister Sarah.

John with the sticking-out ears had the measles.

The twins next door – James and Gerald – had the measles. They had the same brown hair, the same brown eyes, and now they both had the same brown spots.

Mark's friend, Mousey, had the measles. Mousey had so many freckles everyone was surprised that measles could find any room on him.

Have YOU had spotty measles?

"Mousey must be even more spotted than I am," said Mark.

"Mousey must be more spotted than *anyone*," Sarah said. "He is a rare spotted mouse."

"It's worse for me," said Mark. "No one can have a birthday when they are covered in spots."

"No one would be able to come," said Sarah. "Do you feel sick, Mark?"

"I feel a bit sick," said Mark. "Even if I *could* have a birthday, I don't think I would want it."

"That is the worst thing," said Sarah. "Not even *wanting* a birthday is worst of all."

Two days later, when the birthday really came, Mark did not feel sick any more. He just felt spotty.

He opened his presents at breakfast.

His mother and father had given him a camera. It was small, but it would take real pictures. Sarah gave him a paintbox. (She always gave him a paintbox. Whenever Mark got a new paintbox, he gave Sarah the old one.)

All morning they painted.

"It feels funny today," said Mark. "It doesn't feel like a birthday. It doesn't feel special at all."

Sarah had painted a class of children. Now she began to paint spots on them.

Lunch was plain and healthy.

In the afternoon Mark's mother started to brush him all over. She brushed his hair. She brushed his dressing-gown, though it was new and did not need brushing. She brushed his slippers.

"We will have a birthday drive," she said. "The car windows will stop the measles from getting out."

They drove out into the country and up a hill that Mark knew. "There's Peter's house," he said. "Peter-up-the-hill! He has measles, too."

"We might pay him a visit for a moment," Mark's mother said. "He won't catch measles from you if he has them already."

The front door was open. They rang the bell and walked in. Then Mark got a real surprise! The room was full of people. Lots of the people were boys wearing dressing-gowns – all of them spotty boys, MEASLE-Y boys.

"Happy birthday! Happy birthday!" they shouted.

There was John with the sticking-out ears. His ears were still a bit spotty around the edges. There were the twins, James and Gerald. Measles made them look more like each other than ever before. There was Mousey. You could not tell where his freckles left off and his measles began. There was Peter-up-the-hill in a pink dressing-gown, and Peter-next-to-the-shop in a bluey-green one.

"Happy birthday! Happy birthday!" they all shouted.

"It's a measle party," Mark's mother explained. "So many people are getting over measles we decided to have a measle party on your birthday."

"Have you brought my birthday cake?" asked Mark.

"It is in a tin box in the back of the car," said his mother. "I would not forget an important thing like that."

What a funny, spotty, measle-y party! All the guests except Sarah were wearing dressing-gowns.

They played a game called Painting Spots on an Elephant. They played Measle-y Chairs (this is like Musical Chairs except that people who play it have to have the measles).

Sarah found a piece of blue chalk and drew spots all over her face. "I've got *blue* measles," she said. "Mine are very unusual spots." (She did not like being the only person without any spots at all.)

Then came the party food. They had spaghetti and meatballs. They had fruit salad and ice cream, and glasses of orange juice. The fruit salad had strawberries and grapes in it.

Then Mark's mother brought in the cake she had made. It was iced with white icing, and it was spotted and dotted and spattered with pink dots.

"Measles!" cried Mark. "The cake's got measles!" He thought it was the funniest, nicest cake he had ever seen. The measles made it taste extremely delicious.

A measle cake for a measle party! A spotty cake for a dotty party!

"I don't think I'll have a piece of cake," said Sarah. "I don't feel very well . . . I feel all hot and cross."

"Heigh-ho!" said Mark's mother. "I think I know what is wrong."

"You are probably getting the measles," said Mark. "Perhaps *you* will have a measle party too."

"We will think of something else for Sarah," said his mother. "But now we must go home."

"Can't I have a measle party as well?" Sarah pleaded. "I want one, too."

"Measle parties are like comets," said Mark's mother. "If you see one in twenty years you are lucky."

She took Mark and Sarah home, with Mark thinking to himself that it was worth getting the measles at birthday time if a special measles party was the result.

After all, not many people have been to one.

DOCTOR BOOX
AND THE SORE GIRAFFE

Andrew Davies

My friend Doctor Boox, the animal doctor, lives in a big house with rather a lot of animals: dogs, cats, lizards, goats, and so on. Doctor Boox is not the cleverest man in the world, but he does his best. Well, this is the story about Boox and the sore giraffe.

One morning, rather late, Doctor Boox was lying in bed with a few dogs and hamsters, when the telephone rang.

"Boox here," said Boox. "What do you want?"

"Schmitt itty shoo shah," said the telephone.

"Can't hear a word you're saying," said Boox. This was because he had his stethoscope stuck in his ears. He always kept it there to be on the safe side. He took it off and gave it to a dog to hold.

"This is the zoo," said the telephone. "We've got a sore giraffe here."

"Where is it sore?" said Boox.

"In the neck," said the man on the telephone.

"Oh dear," said Boox. "I was afraid of that."

"Well, can you help?"

"Oh, I'll have a go," said Boox. He put the phone down.

"Right, lads," said Boox to the dogs. "We're off to the zoo."

"Row! Row! Row!" shouted the dogs.

They went downstairs to Doctor Boox's red sports car and they all got in. Three of the dogs sat on Boox's knee.

"Move over, lads," said Boox. "Let the dog see the rabbit." And then they were off. Boox drove very fast because it was an emergency.

On the way, he had an idea. He was no fool, and as he had not had dealings with any giraffes before, he thought he would practise on a lamp-post. So he parked his car by one of the biggest lamp-posts in town.

"Let's see," said Boox. And he took a quick run at the lamp-post and went up it in three jumps and a scramble.

"Easy!" said Boox. "Pretty good, eh lads?" But when he looked down at the dogs in the car they seemed a long way down and Doctor Boox began to get frightened. He clung very tight to the lamp-post.

"Row! Row! Row!" shouted the dogs. They wanted him to get down, but Boox didn't know how to get down.

Just then, a policeman came along.

"What are you doing up there?" he said.

"Training," said Boox. "I've got to get up a giraffe this morning."

"A likely tale," said the policeman. "Get down at once!"

"I can't," said Boox. "I'm frightened." So the policeman went away and got the fire brigade. Soon the red fire engine came along.

"I thought you were never coming," said Boox.

The firemen hoisted the big ladder, and Boox stepped very carefully onto it.

"Thanks very much," he said. Then he had another idea.

"I'll tell you what," he said. "What about taking me to the zoo?"

"All right," said the firemen, who had nothing better to do that morning.

So all the dogs got in the fire engine, and the firemen drove to the zoo, with Boox still on the ladder.

"This is the life," said Boox to himself, as they whizzed through the town with the bells ringing.

When they got to the zoo they drove straight up to the giraffe, who was very sore indeed now, and rather cross. But Boox got out his bottle of liniment (on the label it said: DOCTOR BOOX'S DOUBLE STRENGTH NECK RUB) and rubbed the giraffe's neck with it. After a bit the giraffe said,
"Ahhhhh."

"He's better now," said Boox.

"Thank you very much," said the zoo man.

"Good old Boox," said the firemen.

"Row! Row! Row!" said the dogs.

"Don't mention it," said Boox. "Anybody like to come back to my house for a snack?"

They all got into the fire engine and went back to Doctor Boox's house where they all had lemonade and three biscuits each out of Doctor Boox's big biscuit barrel.

Except Boox.

Boox had five biscuits because he thought he owed it to himself after his busy morning.

FUSSY

Anne Fine

Fussy was tired. His eyes were drooping and his thumb kept creeping into his mouth. But before he could go to bed he had to find his special yellow blanket.

And then he needed Elephant with his big flappy ears, in case he was lonely.

And then he needed the huge shiny picture book you could wipe clean, in case he wanted to look at the pictures.

And he wanted his mobile planes spinning round and round above his head–

No! He wanted them stopped.

And then Fussy wanted some water in the cup with the top with the little holes, in case he was thirsty.

And he wanted the fat round pebble he found on the beach one day.

And he wanted the curtains closed so he couldn't see the creepy wavy branches on the tree outside the window–

No! He wanted them open so he *could* see the creepy wavy branches on the tree outside the window.

And he wanted his family of pink rabbits, and all his furry glove puppets, and his bright wooden bricks.

And he wanted his light off–

How many toys go to bed with you? Don't leave anyone behind!

No! He wanted his light back on again.

And he wanted his telephone with the long red loopy wire, and his sailing boat, and his zoo animals, and the shiny winter jacket Gran bought him on Saturday, and his green plastic frog, and his truck and his toy cars, and his pretend bottle of beer.

And then, at last, everything was *just right*. It was exactly how he wanted it. So Fussy shut his eyes and fell asleep.

Phew!

He slept for two whole hours. First he rolled all the way over. Then he rolled all the way back. Then he kicked about a bit.

So the rabbit family got all mixed up with the furry glove puppets. And the bright wooden bricks fell into the back of the truck. And the long red loopy wire of the telephone tangled in the boat's sails. And the toy cars slid down the sleeves of the shiny winter jacket Gran bought him on Saturday. And the fat round pebble he found on the beach one day knocked over the huge shiny picture book you could wipe clean, so it fell on the green plastic frog. And water dripped out of the holes in the top of the cup onto the heads of all the animals from his zoo.

And Elephant practically disappeared under the yellow blanket with the pretend bottle of beer . . .

What a mess! What a terrible mess! It certainly wasn't just right any more. It wasn't how Fussy wanted it at all.

But when he woke up, did he mind? No. Not a bit!

You see, he wasn't fussy any more.

He'd had his nap!

ALFIE
MAKES A SPLASH

Willy Smax

Mike McCannick walked into Smallbills Garage carrying a large can of 20/50 motor oil.

"Yum, yum!" said Benny. "My favourite."

"Sorry, Benny, but it's not for you," said Mike. "It's for Roland Royce. He's coming in for a service."

"I never get anything nice," grumbled Benny.

"That's because you're a dirty old breakdown truck," said Francis Ford Popular. "Expensive oil is only for posh cars like Roland Royce and me."

"If you're posh then I'm a pushchair," said Benny.

"That's enough, you two," said Mike. "Time for work, Benny. We've got to pick up some spare parts for Roland."

They drove off to the car spares shop.

"Oh, oh!" said Mike, looking in his rear-view mirror. "Look who's coming up behind us."

It was Alfie the sports car, flashing his lights to overtake.

"You're going too fast," said Benny when they stopped together at the next junction.

"Oh, shut up," said Alfie. "I'm in a hurry. I'm going to take a short cut."

The lights changed and he shot out through a small gap in the traffic, nearly causing an accident.

"Hey! Don't go down there!" shouted Benny. "It's . . ."

Alfie didn't wait to listen. He shot off down a slip road, going so fast he didn't see that it went straight down to the canal.

There was a huge SPLASH as Alfie hit the water.

"Help! Help!" he shouted. "I'm drowning!"

"Oh no!" said Mike. "Alfie's fallen in!"

Benny had a bright idea. He whizzed up the road, turned on to the bridge and reversed up to the railings. He lowered his big hook so that it caught under Alfie's bumper, and pulled him up through the air dripping with water.

A crowd had gathered and everyone cheered as Benny lifted Alfie over the railings. Then Benny proudly towed Alfie home.

Back at the garage Mike cleaned out Alfie's carburettor and charged up his battery. By the end of the day Alfie was feeling fine.

"I'm sorry I was rude to you, Benny," said Alfie. "Thank you for saving my life."

"That's OK," said Benny. "That's my job."

"Benny, I think you deserve a reward," said Mike, and he picked up the big can of 20/50 motor oil. Slowly he poured the thick golden oil into Benny's engine.

Francis Ford Popular couldn't believe his headlamps when he saw Benny glugging down Roland Royce's favourite drink.

"But that's only for posh cars like me and Roland," he said.

"Posh cars – and heroes," said Alfie.

"That's right," said Mike, getting ready to go home. "Goodnight, Benny! Goodnight, Alfie!" He looked over to Francis. "And goodnight to you, your royal highness."

Find out how Benny helps Morton the naughty motorbike on page 189!

NETTIE'S
NEW HOUSE

Lynda Britnell

Nettie Mugwort the fairy lived in a hollow log in the forest.

All summer her friends came to visit her there – Know-It-All the gnome, Bluebell the fairy, and Mr Beechtree who owned the sweet shop.

During the day the friends would sit and have tea and honeycakes, and in the evening they would watch the sun go down.

But as summer came to an end the weather got colder. The wind blew leaves and twigs into Nettie's home. The rain blew in and made her mats and chairs wet, and her friends didn't like coming to visit her because it was so cold inside the log.

One morning Bluebell came to see Nettie.

"Good morning, Nettie," said Bluebell, but Nettie didn't answer. She was sitting in a chair holding a cup of tea and sniffing loudly.

"Oh, Nettie, what is the matter?" asked Bluebell.

"I don't feel well," said Nettie, rubbing her red nose. "All night long it rained and the wind blew, and now I've got a horrible cold."

"We will have to find you a new warm home," said Bluebell. "Come along."

So Nettie and Bluebell went off to find Nettie a new home.

The town was full of toadstool houses. Some were small with flat tops. Some were middle-sized with domed tops. Some were large with spotted tops.

Nettie stood beside a small flat-topped toadstool. "This is no good," said Nettie, "I'm taller than the roof of this house."

Then Nettie and Bluebell went to see a middle-sized toadstool with a domed roof.

"This is bigger," said Bluebell.

"Yes, it is," said Nettie, "but I will have to crawl through the front door. It is still not big enough."

156

Next they went to a large toadstool with a high spotted roof.

"This will be big enough," said Bluebell.

Nettie could just get through the door but when she tried to stand up straight inside the toadstool . . . BOMP! She hit her head on the ceiling.

"Oh dear," said Bluebell. "We don't have any bigger toadstools. Where are you going to live?"

The two friends walked sadly to Mr Beechtree's sweet shop. Bluebell told Mr Beechtree how all the toadstools were too small.

"Have you looked at the old oak tree across the path?" said Mr Beechtree. "No one has lived there for a long time because it is too big."

Nettie, Bluebell and Mr Beechtree hurried to the old oak tree.

Mr Beechtree pushed open the door. The doorway was much bigger than Nettie, so she didn't have to crawl in. And the ceiling was much higher, so she didn't bang her head. Nettie looked around and smiled.

"This will be my new home," she said.

Know-It-All, Bluebell and Mr Beechtree all helped Nettie carry her table and chairs, her plates and cups and her bed into the old oak tree.

When they had put everything safely in her new home, Nettie and her friends had a lovely tea of lemonade and honeycakes.

And Nettie Mugwort has lived in the old oak tree ever since.

Can you remember how Nettie got her name?

How the Wizard's Hat Became

Sue Inman

In the old days, wizards used to wear all sorts of different hats. They wore tophats, sunhats, pom-pom hats; in fact any kind of hat would do for a wizard then. But something happened to change all that . . .

Wizard Otto received an invitation:

The King and Queen
are pleased to invite
Otto the Wizard
to a Royal Ball on Saturday Night
PS Please bring a banana and don't be late

"Prince Charming and his sister Princess Rose will be there," thought Otto. He was secretly in love with Princess Rose. "Maybe," he thought, "just maybe, if I look my very best, Princess Rose will dance with me!"

So Otto decided to make himself a brand new hat. He made it from a breakfast cereal packet. It was tall and pointed, and Otto painted it blue. But when he tried it on, he didn't like it.

"It's too dull and boring," he said to himself. "It needs brightening up."

Otto decided to decorate his new hat. He cut some circles out of brightly coloured paper and stuck them on.

"That's better," he said with a smile. Otto was very pleased with his new hat, and he went to bed a happy wizard.

But in the night, a Bad Fairy came. She stole the circles right off Otto's new hat.

So, in the morning, Otto decided to try a different shape. A shape the Bad Fairy would not steal. He thought squares might look nice so he cut some out and decorated his hat with them.

"Wow, they look terrific," he said, admiring the new hat in the mirror. "Much better than the circles."

That night, while Otto was in bed, the Bad Fairy came again. She stole all the squares from Otto's new hat.

When Otto discovered what had happened, he said, "I've had enough of this, I'm going to sort that Bad Fairy out, once and for all!" Then he marched straight out of his front door and he didn't stop marching until he got to the Bad Fairy's house.

Otto knocked on the Bad Fairy's door.

"Who's there?" called the Bad Fairy.

"Otto the Wizard," said Otto the Wizard.

"Uh-oh," said the Bad Fairy, but she let him in anyway.

In the Bad Fairy's house, Otto saw something amazing. The Bad Fairy was making herself a new dress. Onto this dress she had sewn Otto's shapes.

"What's going on here?" said Otto.

The Bad Fairy explained, "You see, I'm going to a party on Saturday night and I want to be the prettiest fairy at the ball. Prince Charming will be there, and . . ." She was too embarrassed to tell Otto what she hoped might happen when she danced with Prince Charming.

Otto the Wizard nodded understandingly. "I see," he said, trying to look suitably cross. Just then he noticed something in the corner of the Bad Fairy's room. It was a wastepaper basket, and it was overflowing with different shapes. There was every shape you can imagine in that bin, and all sorts of different colours.

"I've tried all those on my dress," said the Bad Fairy. "But none of them looked very nice. I like your shapes best."

"Well, in that case," said Otto, "I have an idea. Why don't you keep my shapes and I'll see if I can find some new ones I like in your bin?"

Otto was delighted to find such a lot of lovely shapes in the bin. There were so many, it was hard for him to decide which ones he liked best. In the end he chose some gold stars and some silver moons. He took the stars and moons home with him and he stuck them on his hat. It looked wonderful, and Otto was very pleased.

When Saturday arrived, Otto the Wizard put on his beautiful new hat, picked up a banana, and set off for the party, hoping that Princess Rose would dance with him. The Bad Fairy set off for the party too. She was hoping that Prince Charming would dance with her. She certainly did look very pretty.

But she never arrived at the party. On her way there, she slipped on a banana skin that someone had carelessly dropped on the path. She skidded over and landed in a muddy puddle. Her beautiful new dress was completely ruined, and she ran home in tears.

What kind of hats do YOU like wearing?

So the Prince spent all night dancing with a stranger. Nobody knew her name, but she did have a beautiful pair of glass slippers.

As for Otto, he enjoyed the party very much. Princess Rose danced with him three times, and all the other wizards admired his hat enormously. In fact his hat was so admired that he decided to make lots more just the same to give to his friends. And all the wizards who were not Otto's friends, and who didn't receive one of the wonderful hats, copied it anyway.

And that is why, if you should meet a wizard nowadays, you can be sure that he will be wearing a tall blue hat decorated with stars and moons.

HUFFING AND PUFFING

Vivian French

Dear Mother,

I do hope you are well. I am, and I have been eating my spinach like you told me to. I hope it is making me strong because – guess what? – tomorrow I am going to a Huffing and Puffing class! I am going to learn how to huff and puff and blow a house down.

Love Wolfie
x x x

Dear Mother,

Today I went to my first ever Huffing and Puffing class. There is a big wolf called Hunk, and when it was my turn to huff he laughed and it put me off. Hunk says he is the best huffer and puffer in the whole world. Hunk says he can blow a straw house down with one puff! He says he can blow a stick house down with two puffs! He says he can blow a brick house down as easy as winking!

Love Wolfie x x x

Dear Mother,

Thank you for the extra spinach. I had two helpings for breakfast. I will try not to let Hunk put me off, but it is very difficult. I wish I was big like he is.

Love Wolfie x x x

Dear Mother,

Guess what? I went to my class today and Hunk said, "Hullo, Tiddler!" He said if I wanted I could go out with him and see him blow a house down!!!!! I think I will learn a lot.

Excitedly,
Wolfie xxx

Dear Mother,

Hunk called for me this morning very early. I hadn't eaten my breakfast, but Hunk said it didn't matter because I would have something much nicer to eat by the end of the day. I said, was it spinach? and he laughed and said, "Good joke, Tiddler!" I didn't know what he meant.

We walked up and down and round and round and then – guess what? There was the neatest little straw house right by the side of the path!

"Now," said Hunk, "watch me blow it down with just one puff!" And he laughed. It wasn't a very nice laugh. And do you know what? When I saw the house I didn't want Hunk to blow it down.

Hunk wouldn't listen, though. He huffed and he puffed and he huffed and he puffed – and the straw house fell to bits! And a little piglet ran out crying. I was so sorry for him. Hunk ran after him, but the little piglet ran faster and Hunk couldn't catch him. When Hunk came back he said, "There you are, Tiddler! That's the way to do it! Just one puff!" I didn't say that I had been counting, and he had huffed and puffed at least ten times.

I wanted to go home then, but Hunk said I was to come and see him blow down a house of sticks with two puffs. He looked so fierce I didn't like to say no. We went up and down and round and round, and sure enough! There was a dear little house of sticks. I said, "PLEASE don't blow it down," but Hunk growled, "Be quiet!" Then he huffed and puffed and huffed and puffed until he was red in the face – and suddenly

CRASH!!!

the little stick house fell to bits . . . and out ran two little pigs! Hunk chased after them but he was too slow.

"There you are, Tiddler!" he said when he came back. "Two puffs! Two puffs – and down it goes!" I didn't know what to say. Hunk was telling a great big fib! He'd huffed and puffed lots and lots and lots!

Hunk didn't notice I didn't say anything. He took my arm and dragged me along the path.

"Time for the brick house, Tiddler!" he said. "And this time I'll catch those little pigs! I'll catch them – and I'll eat them!"

Wasn't that terrible, Mother? I knew then that Hunk was a very bad wolf. I wanted to run away but I couldn't. He was holding my paw.

The little brick house was the nicest of all. It had a bright red front door and a tall chimney on the top.

Hunk ran to the house and began to huff and puff. He huffed and puffed and huffed and puffed until he was purple, but he could not blow that little brick house down. I was so pleased! But then he said, "Now then, Tiddler! I've got a job for you!!" And he picked me up and he put me on the roof! I was shocked!

"Put me down!" I said.

"Why do you think I brought you here, you horrible little weed?" Hunk growled. "Get down that chimney – or else!" And he showed his teeth. They were ever so sharp! Before I knew what I was doing I scrambled up the chimney and slid down inside with a WHOOOMPH!

The three little pigs were so surprised! They just stared and stared! I said I was really really sorry, and I said Hunk wasn't my friend. I said I was very very sorry about the straw house and the stick house, and I did hope they could mend them. I was beginning to explain about the Huffing and Puffing classes when there was a strange noise above our heads. We all looked up, and guess what! Hunk was trying to get down the chimney!

I looked at the three little pigs, and they looked at me.

"Quick!" said the first little pig, and he and the other two began scurrying round putting sticks in the fireplace. Then they put a big pan of water on top of the sticks, and lit the sticks . . . and the water in the pan began to bubble and boil . . . exactly under the chimney.

"I think," I said, "he's too fat to get down."

"Better safe than sorry," said the second little pig.

"Look!" said the third little pig, and she pointed. There was Hunk's tail, hanging down!

Mother, I am not a good little wolf. I am not a very bad wolf like Hunk, but I am not good. I did a terrible thing. When I saw Hunk's tail hanging down like that I thought about him pretending to be my friend when he was just wanting to put me down a chimney. I thought about him spoiling those dear little houses and scaring those nice little pigs. I picked up a burning stick and I burnt his tail!

Howwwww L !

Hunk was out of that chimney and off and away as if his tail was alight. Well, if I am a truthful little wolf, Mother, it was. The three little pigs cheered and cheered.

Mother, I am not going back to Huffing and Puffing classes. I don't want to blow houses down. I am going to visit the three little pigs on Mondays, Wednesday and Fridays, and they are going to teach me how to build houses. I think I will like that much much better.

Love (lots) from
Wolfie x x x

PIGGO HAS A TRAIN RIDE

Pam Ayres

One of the nicest things about where Piggo lived was the red steam train which took visitors for long rides around the whole park. Piggo had hardly ever seen it properly, because just as it passed the pen where he lived with his mum and all the other piglets, it went behind a fence. He just caught a glimpse of the shiny red engine, and the line of children smiling and waving before they all disappeared. Then he would hear the train whistle blow twice – TOOT TOOT – before the sound of the engine died away. Piggo wished he could see it properly, or better still, ride on it with the children.

One afternoon Piggo was restless. His mum and all his brothers and sisters had gone to sleep in a big pile in the sunshine. Piggo wasn't tired. He was just wondering what to do when he heard hooves. It was Jacob, the spotty lamb.

"Hello," he said to Piggo, "coming for a walk?"

Just what Piggo wanted! He told his mum, then in one jump he cleared the pigsty wall. Together he and Jacob trotted out of the farmyard to see what they could find. First they walked all along the shallow stream. Fat white ducks waddled and fussed about in the water. Then they went over the bridge. Peering down through the railings they could see fish in the water, keeping quite still but for an occasional swish of their tails.

"I'm hungry," said Piggo.

"So am I," agreed Jacob.

Far away on the steep hillside they could see some large ginger cows with long horns.

"We'll go and ask the cows for some of their food," Jacob decided. He leapt in the air and galloped off towards them, his black hooves flying.

Piggo was getting tired. His legs ached. He wished he had long white bouncy legs like Jacob instead of short pink stiff legs. Wearily he plodded up the hill towards the cows.

172

"Well, yes," the brown cow was nodding, "you and your friend *can* have some of our lunch. It's cow nuts today. It's cow nuts most days. Over there, look, in the big white bowl."

"Thank you," chorused Piggo and Jacob, crunching gratefully. "Thank you very much."

After lunch Jacob raced round the field and jumped over Piggo a few times. Piggo sat down beside a white fence and stared sadly across the park to the Children's Farmyard. His home in the friendly pigsty seemed so far away, back down the hill, over the bridge, all along the stream. Jacob seemed to be able to bounce for ever. Piggo felt very worried and gloomy. He had come too far. His trotters were weary from walking and he wanted his mum.

TOOT! TOOT! TOOT! TOOT! Piggo sat up. What was that?

TOOT! TOOT! Piggo knew that sound! It was the steam train! Suddenly it appeared, coming merrily along the track on the other side of the white fence. How smashing it looked, with its red engine shining and big puffs of steam billowing up from the funnel. Then the brakes began to screech and the little train puffed to a halt. All the children were looking ahead as the driver called back to them.

"Here are the Highland Cattle," he was saying. "Can you see their big horns?"

A magnificent idea came to Piggo. Of course! The steam train went right past his home!

"Come on, Jacob!" called Piggo excitedly, and together they jumped the white picket fence and scrambled up onto one of the red leather seats. Piggo was thrilled! At last, he was having a ride on the steam train!

"All aboard for the Children's Farmyard!" called the driver. "Hold tight now."

And off they went – TOOT TOOT! TOOT TOOT! – with Piggo and Jacob in the last seat of all, looking *very* excited, and having a ride all the way home.

Piggo has a friend called Edgar. Have you heard his story yet?

FLYING FELIX

Michael Lawrence

Felix the Caterpillar lay in the grass watching Milly and Molly the Mayfly twins flying about overhead.

"Felix!" they called. "Why don't you come and play with us?"

"Can't," Felix answered grumpily. "Haven't got any wings."

So Milly and Molly flew off to find someone else to play with.

Winston the Wasp came by.

"Lovely day for a fly!" he said. "Or a wasp for that matter." And he buzzed off, chortling.

Then along came Hugh the Housefly, whirring his wings like billy-o.

"I know I should be in the house," Hugh said, "but it's much too fine a day to be stuck indoors," and he whirred happily away.

Felix gazed after him.

"Wish I could fly," he thought.

Nearby, under a toadstool, sat Betty the Snail.

"Can you fly, Betty?" Felix said.

Betty laughed.

"Of course not. Snails don't fly!" And she went back into her shell.

It seemed to Felix that flying must be the best thing in all the world.

"Perhaps you don't have to have wings to fly," he said to himself.

He closed his eyes, curled his tail under him, took a deep breath, jumped into the air, and – fell straight back down again!

But Felix wasn't a caterpillar to give up easily. He looked at the grass growing all round him.

"I'm sure I could fly from the top of one of those blades of grass," he said.

So he began crawling up a blade of grass.

Lottie the Ladybird flew by.

"You mind you don't fall off, young caterpillar. You could hurt yourself."

"I'm going to fly," Felix told her proudly.

"I don't think you are, dear," Lottie answered, and went off to find Felix's mum.

Felix crawled to the very tip of the blade of grass and got ready. But as he stood there, the grass trembled. And so did Felix. The grass shook. So did Felix.

And instead of flying off the blade of grass, he fell straight into a puddle.

When he looked up his mother was standing over him.

"And what are you up to, my lad?" she asked.

"I was trying to fly," Felix replied.

"One day," his mother told him, "you'll turn into a butterfly like me. Then you'll fly, but not before."

When he was alone again, Felix gazed at himself in the puddle, and sighed.

"*One* day I'll fly. *One* day." And then he said, "But what can I do *today*?"

"Whoops!"

Felix looked up. Cedric the Centipede had fallen over his feet again.

"You don't know how lucky you are, Felix," Cedric said. "I have a hundred feet to fall over and you have hardly any. I wish *I* was a caterpillar."

Felix watched Cedric trot away, tripping over his feet every few steps.

"I suppose I am quite lucky really," he said.

And he climbed onto a leaf, curled himself up in the warm sunshine, and went to sleep.

BILLY, THE UNBELIEVABLY GREEDY BABY

Paul and Emma Rogers

Right from the day he was born, Billy Buzoni ate enough food for twenty babies and more. He'd have potatoes, porridge, plums, bread, bananas, beans, soup, spaghetti and ice cream – and that was only his breakfast.

Billy ate seven meals a day – and snacks in between. Everyone thought he was the greediest baby they'd ever met. Poor Mr and Mrs Buzoni didn't know what to do. As soon as Billy learned to grab, they hardly dared take him out shopping.

Once Billy started to crawl, they had to put a padlock on the fridge. And within a week of his learning to walk, they had to keep the food on the highest shelf in the larder.

At the end of a meal, it was no good saying, "No more now." A few minutes later they'd find Billy munching a magazine or chewing up flowers outside.

One day Mr Buzoni came in from the garden and called to Mrs Buzoni, "You know the rabbit's been getting thinner. Well, guess who's been enjoying its dinner?"

In the end, they were so worried they took Billy along to the hospital. But while they were talking to the doctor, he got into the hospital kitchen. Lots of the patients went hungry that day . . .

Billy Buzoni was eating his family out of house and home. Mrs Buzoni stared at the empty larder. There was only one lettuce leaf left on the shelf. They were down to their last stick of spaghetti. They had only a few pennies left to spend. What were they going to do?

Then, on the way to the supermarket, they saw a notice:

For a moment, both the Buzonis thought, "How very silly!" Then their eyes met and in one breath they cried, "We'll enter Billy!"

The very next day they started Billy's training. It was hard work for his mum and dad, but life for Billy was wonderful – just one meal after another!

In between, they took him for long walks to build up his appetite. And after each meal, when Billy appeared to have finished, instead of saying, "Quick! Let's hide what's left from his sight!", they begged, "You can do it, Billy, just one more bite!"

"Funny," Billy thought, "I wonder why it's pancakes again tonight?"

This story is making me hungry!

The day of the competition came. A huge crowd had gathered. Poor Billy hadn't eaten all day. Mr and Mrs Buzoni sat him at the table. At last they heard the umpire say, "All right. No resting. No one must cheat. You must keep going. Ready . . . Steady . . . Eat!"

Cynthia Stodge got off to a good start, stuffing them in four at a time . . . And Big Bob was washing them down with mouthfuls of beer . . . The crowd cheered. The cooks kept the pancakes coming . . .

But what was this? Big Bob was slowing down! And Cynthia was falling asleep!

"Come on!" the crowd shouted. "You mustn't stop yet! You've got to win. We've all made a bet!"

But Big Bob wasn't looking too good.

"Oh, my tummy," he groaned. "I feel so ill. I can't eat any more – but that baby will!"

Mr Buzoni just smiled to his wife and whispered, "Keep munching, Bill."

The crowd kept count as the pancakes disappeared.

"A hundred and two? It can't be true! Two hundred and four! He's asking for more!"

The umpire stood up.

"He's only a baby," he said. "Just a beginner. But I declare Billy Buzoni the winner!"

Mr and Mrs Buzoni gave Billy a big hug – very carefully. The umpire presented them with a cheque for a thousand pounds. He asked the Buzonis what they'd do with the money. Take a holiday? Buy a car?

Mr Buzoni replied, "We might have a treat or two, maybe, but most of the prize will buy food for the baby!"

That night the Buzonis went to the best restaurant in town to celebrate. They ordered the grandest meal on the menu – fresh lobster, roast beef, raspberry sorbet, trifle and cheese.

And Billy – couldn't eat a thing.

GOLDILOCKS AND THE THREE BEARS

Vivian French

There were once three bears who lived in a house in the middle of a wood. There was a great big daddy bear, a middle-sized mummy bear, and a little teeny baby bear as well. Every morning they made porridge for breakfast, and every morning they went out for a walk while the porridge cooled.

One day when the three bears were out walking, a little girl came hurrying up the path to their house. She had been picking flowers in the wood and had lost her way, and she knocked on the door to ask which path would take her home.

BANG! BANG! BANG!

The little girl knocked very loudly, but no one answered. "H'm," she said to herself, "maybe they're all asleep." And she turned the handle.

The door opened at once. The three bears never locked it, because no one had ever come to that part of the wood before. The little girl pushed the door open wide.

"Is anyone there?" she called out. "I'm Goldilocks, and I've lost my way!"

There was still no answer, so she walked right into the neat and tidy kitchen . . . .

and there, on the table in front of her, were three steaming bowls of porridge. There was a great big bowl, a middle-sized bowl and a little teeny bowl.

"Oh!" said Goldilocks, and her eyes shone. "Porridge! I love porridge! And I'm so hungry! I'm sure they'd never notice if I ate just a spoonful or two." And she picked up the great big spoon and dipped it into the great big bowl.

"EEEEK! OWWWWW!"

said Goldilocks. "This porridge is much too hot!

Maybe I'll try the middle-sized bowl instead." And she picked up the middle-sized spoon and dipped it into the middle-sized bowl.

"UGH! YUCK!"

said Goldilocks. "This porridge is much too cold!

Maybe I'll try the little teeny bowl instead." And she picked up the little teeny spoon and dipped it into the little teeny bowl.

"YUM! YUM! YUM!"

said Goldilocks. "This porridge is JUST RIGHT!"

And before she knew what she was doing she had eaten it all up.

"Oh dear," said Goldilocks when she saw what she had done. "Oh dear – but it did taste so delicious!" She gave a little teeny yawn. "I'm tired. Maybe I'll sit down for a moment or two." And she climbed up into the great big chair for a rest.

The great big chair was not very comfortable. Goldilocks wriggled and twisted about, and at last she climbed out again.

"That chair is much too hard," she said. "No one could rest in there. I'll try the middle-sized chair." And she scrambled into the soft pink cushions of the middle-sized chair . . . but that was no good either.

"That chair is much too soft," said Goldilocks. "I'll try the little teeny chair." And she scrambled out of the middle-sized chair.

"Ummmm . . ." said Goldilocks as she sat herself down on the little teeny chair. "That is so comfortable!" She yawned a middle-sized yawn as she rocked herself to and fro and to and fro until . . .

CRASH!

the little teeny chair fell into pieces round her.

"Oh dear, oh dear," said Goldilocks as she picked herself up. "I didn't mean to break it . . . really I didn't." And she yawned again . . . a great big yawn. "I wonder if there's a cosy bed upstairs?"

Goldilocks went slowly up the stairs, and sure enough there was a bedroom with three beds in it. There was a great big bed, a middle-sized bed and a little teeny bed. Goldilocks climbed into the great big bed, but it was much too hard. Then she scrambled into the soft pink pillows of the middle-sized bed, but that was much too soft.

"I can't sleep in either of those beds," Goldilocks said crossly. "I'll try the little teeny bed.

UMMMMMMMMMMMMMMMMM!"

said Goldilocks as she snuggled down in the little teeny bed. "This is so comfortable . . ." and in no time at all she was fast asleep.

Not long after Goldilocks had fallen asleep the three bears came back from their walk. They were surprised to find the door wide open and they hurried inside.

"GOODNESS ME!" said the great big daddy bear in a great big voice as he looked at the table. "LOOK AT THIS! SOMEONE'S BEEN EATING MY PORRIDGE!"

"GOODNESS ME!" said the middle-sized mummy bear in a middle-sized voice. "LOOK AT THIS! SOMEONE'S BEEN EATING MY PORRIDGE!"

"GOODNESS ME!" said the little teeny baby bear in a little teeny voice. "LOOK AT THIS! SOMEONE'S BEEN EATING MY PORRIDGE, AND THEY'VE EATEN IT ALL UP!"

The great big daddy bear walked over to the three chairs, and he scratched his ears.

"FANCY THAT!" he said in his great big voice.
"SOMEONE'S BEEN SITTING
IN MY CHAIR!"

The middle-sized mummy bear scratched her nose.

"FANCY THAT!" she said in her middle-sized voice.
"SOMEONE'S BEEN SITTING
IN *MY* CHAIR!"

The little teeny baby bear scratched his tummy.

"FANCY THAT!" he said in his little teeny voice.

"SOMEONE'S BEEN SITTING IN *MY* CHAIR, AND THEY'VE BROKEN IT!"

The great big daddy bear went stumping up the stairs to the bedroom.

"WELL I NEVER!" said the great big daddy bear in his great big voice. "SOMEONE'S BEEN SLEEPING IN MY BED!"

The middle-sized mummy bear hurried up the stairs after the great big daddy bear.

"WELL I NEVER!" she said in her middle-sized voice. "SOMEONE'S BEEN SLEEPING IN *MY* BED!"

The little teeny baby bear rushed up the stairs after the middle-sized mummy bear.

"WELL I NEVER EVER DID!" he said in his little teeny voice. "SOMEONE'S BEEN SLEEPING IN *MY* BED – AND SHE'S STILL HERE FAST ASLEEP!"

And all three bears stood round the bed and stared and stared and stared at Goldilocks until she woke up.

"OH!" said Goldilocks when she saw the bears. "OH! OH! OH!" And she jumped out of the little teeny bed and rushed down the stairs and away out of the bears' little house . . . and she didn't stop running until she reached her very own home.

MORTON AT
THE BUILDING SITE

Willy Smax

Morton the naughty blue motorcycle had spent the whole morning watching the busy building site on the other side of Wrench Road. He thought the red dumper truck was having the most fun, pouring cement into square holes in the ground.

He was so busy watching that he didn't notice Mike arrive with a large package.

"Morning, Morton," said Mike. "Look what I've got for you."

Mike had bought a big blue and white topbox so that Morton could carry his tools when they went out to work together.

"Just what I've always wanted," said Morton, flashing his headlights.

"It's only for carrying tools," said Mike, "so don't go getting into trouble with it."

But Morton couldn't wait to use his brand-new topbox. As soon as Mike had gone, the naughty blue motorcycle sneaked off to the building site across the street. He went straight up to the red dumper truck, who was still pouring cement into square holes.

"I bet *I* could do that," said Morton.

"Oh, yeah?" said the dumper truck.

"Just watch me!" said Morton. He rode up to the cement mixer, filled up his brand-new topbox with a big load of sludgy cement, and carried the cement over to the foundation holes.

"And just how are you going to pour it in, Mister clever bike?" asked the dumper truck.

"Easy peasy," said Morton. "I'll just do a wheelie."

And with a flick of his accelerator, his front wheel leapt into the air, and the cement poured neatly out of his topbox and into one of the holes.

"You'd better be careful doing that," said the dumper truck. "It's muddy here, and you might slip. You wouldn't want to wind up stuck in the cement."

"Not me!" said Morton. "Come on, I bet I can fill up more holes than you can!" And he raced off to get some more cement.

As soon as his topbox was full, he sped back and twisted his throttle to do another wheelie. But he was going much too fast, and he spun head over wheels in the air.

"WHOOO!" screamed Morton as he landed with both wheels stuck in the cement. "Please get Benny to pull me out," he pleaded.

The red dumper truck could hardly stop snickering as he drove off to find Benny.

"Hurry up!" shouted Morton, who could already feel the cement drying on his wheels.

It seemed ages before Benny came, and he couldn't help smiling as he swung his tow-hook under Morton. When he lifted Morton out of the holes, there were two big blocks of cement set on his wheels. Poor Morton was mortified.

CRASH! went Morton as Benny lowered him onto the garage floor. Mike rushed out to see what the noise was about.

"What on earth have you got on your wheels?" shouted Mike.

"Oh, just a little cement," said Morton.

"A little?" said Mike. "You've got half a building there!"

"I know," said Morton sadly. "Do you think you can get it off?"

Mike reached into his toolbox and pulled out the largest hammer and chisel he could find.

"With pleasure!" he said.

NETTIE'S
NEW SHOES

Lynda Britnell

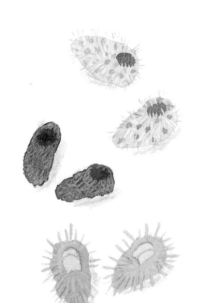

Nettie Mugwort was a fairy.

But Nettie wasn't an ordinary fairy. She was taller than an ordinary fairy. Her hair was spikier than an ordinary fairy's hair, in fact rather like a hedgehog. And Nettie's feet were bigger than an ordinary fairy's feet. In fact, Nettie's feet were three times bigger than an ordinary fairy's feet. And this was a problem because none of the shoe shops had shoes in Nettie's size. All the shoes she tried on were too small.

So Nettie thought, "I will make my own shoes."

She went into the fairy forest with a big bag and collected lots of things. First she made some shoes from dandelion seeds. They looked soft and warm. But when Nettie put the shoes on, sand got in them and tickled her toes.

Next she made some shoes from sweet chestnut shells. They wouldn't let the sand in to tickle her toes. But when Nettie put them on she prickled her fingers.

"Ouch!" she said. "If I trod on someone I would hurt them."

Last of all Nettie made some shoes from moss. They wouldn't hurt if she trod on someone. But when she walked out in the rain the moss got soggy and Nettie's feet got wet.

Nettie sat down. "Oh, what shall I do?" she said.

Just then she heard a thump! thump! thump! It was coming closer: *Thump! thump! thump!* And closer: THUMP! THUMP! THUMP! And closer: *THUMP! THUMP! THUMP!*

Out of the trees came Know-It-All the Gnome. He stopped beside Nettie.

"What's wrong?" he said.

Nettie told him about her problem feet and that she couldn't find any shoes to fit.

"Your feet aren't a problem," said Know-It-All. "Look! Your feet are the same size as mine."

And when Nettie looked she saw that they were.

"You haven't looked in the right place," said Know-It-All. "Come with me."

And that is what she did.

Know-It-All took her to a shop called Gnome Your Feet. Gnome Your Feet was a wonderful place. There were all kinds of shoes: big shoes and little shoes, plain shoes and sparkly shoes.

Nettie found a pair of pink hiking boots that fitted perfectly.

"They may not be as small as other fairies' shoes," said Nettie.

"But they fit," said Know-It-All.

"And I like them," said Nettie.

What colour are YOUR favourite shoes?

THE LITTLE GIRL
AND THE TINY DOLL

Aingelda Ardizzone

There was once a tiny doll who belonged to a girl who did not care for dolls.

For a long time she lay forgotten in a mackintosh pocket until one rainy day when the girl was out shopping. The girl was following her mother round a grocer's shop when she put her hand in her pocket and felt something hard.

She took it out and saw it was the doll. "Ugly old thing," she said and quickly put it back again, as she thought, into her pocket. But, in fact, since she didn't want the doll, she dropped it unnoticed into the deep freeze among the frozen peas.

The tiny doll lay quite still for a long time, wondering what was to become of her. She felt so sad, partly because she did not like being called ugly and partly because she was lost.

It was very cold in the deep freeze and the tiny doll began to feel rather stiff, so she decided to walk about and have a good look at the place. The floor was crisp and white, just like frost on a winter's morning. There were many packets of peas piled one on top of the other.

194

They seemed to her like great big buildings. The cracks between the piles were rather like narrow streets.

She walked one way and then the other, passing not only packets of peas, but packets of sliced beans, spinach, broccoli and mixed vegetables. Then she turned a corner and found herself among beef rissoles and fish fingers. However, she did not stop but went on exploring until she came to boxes of strawberries; and then ice cream.

The strawberries reminded her of the time when she was lost once before among the strawberry plants in a garden. Then she sat all day in the sun smelling and eating strawberries.

Now she made herself as comfortable as possible among the boxes.

The only trouble was that people were continually taking boxes out to buy them and the shop people were always putting in new ones. At times it was very frightening. Once she was nearly squashed by a box of fish fingers.

The tiny doll had no idea how long she spent in the deep freeze. Sometimes it seemed very quiet. This, she supposed, was when the shop was closed for the night. She could not keep count of the days.

One day when she was busy eating ice cream out of a packet, she suddenly looked up and saw a little girl she had never seen before. The little girl was sorry for the tiny doll and wished she could take her home. The doll looked so cold and lonely, but the girl did not dare to pick her up because she had been told not to touch things in the shop. However, she felt she must do something to help the doll and as soon as she got home she set to work to make her some warm clothes.

First of all, she made her a warm bonnet out of a piece of red flannel. This was a nice and easy thing to start with. After tea that day she asked her mother to help her cut out a coat from a piece of blue velvet. She stitched away so hard that she had just time to finish it before she went to bed. It was very beautiful.

The next day her mother said they were going shopping, so the little girl put the coat and bonnet in an empty matchbox and tied it into a neat parcel with brown paper and string. She held the parcel tightly in her hand as she walked along the street. As soon as she reached the shop she ran straight to the deep freeze to look for the tiny doll.

At first she could not see her anywhere. Then, suddenly, she saw her, right at the back, playing with the peas. The tiny doll was throwing them into the air and hitting them with an ice cream spoon.

The little girl threw in the parcel and the doll at once started to untie it. She looked very pleased when she saw what was inside. She tried on the coat, and it fitted. She tried on the bonnet and it fitted too. She jumped up and down with excitement and waved to the little girl to say thank you. She felt so much much better in warm clothes and it made her feel happy to think that somebody cared for her.

Then she had an idea. She made the matchbox into a bed and pretended that the brown paper was a great big blanket. With the string she wove a mat to go beside the bed.

At last she settled down in the matchbox, wrapped herself in the brown paper blanket and went to sleep.

She had a long, long sleep because she was very tired and, when she woke up, she found that the little girl had been back again and had left another parcel. This time it contained a yellow scarf.

Now the little girl came back to the shop every day and each time she brought something new for the tiny doll. She made her a sweater, a petticoat, and knickers with tiny frills, and gave her a little bit of a looking glass to see herself in. She also gave her some red tights which belonged to one of her own dolls to see if they would fit. They fitted perfectly.

At last the tiny doll was beautifully dressed and looked quite cheerful, but still nobody except the little girl ever noticed her.

"Couldn't we ask someone about the doll?" the little girl asked her mother. "I would love to take her home to play with."

The mother said she would ask the lady at the cash desk when they went to pay for their shopping.

"Do you know about the doll in the deep freeze?"

"No indeed," the lady replied. "There are no dolls in this shop."

"Oh yes there are," said the little girl and her mother, both at once. So the lady from the cash desk, the little girl and her mother all marched off to have a look. And there, sure enough, was the tiny doll down among the frozen peas.

"It's not much of a life for a doll in there," said the shop lady, picking up the doll and giving her to the little girl. "You had better take her home where she will be out of mischief."

Having said this, she marched back to her desk with a rather haughty expression.

The little girl took the tiny doll home, where she lived for many happy years in a beautiful dolls' house. The little girl played with her a great deal, but best of all the tiny doll liked the company of the other dolls. They all loved to listen to her adventures in the deep freeze.

THE GREAT
GOOSE HUNT

Selina Young

It was a beautiful sunny day and the bees were buzzing round the hive. Everything was fine and dandy when suddenly Margery the farmer's wife ran out from the yard, screaming and shouting.

"The goose has disappeared! Whatever shall we do?" And she flapped her arms about in the air in despair.

Pete, her husband, came out from the shed where he was chopping wood.

"Whatever's all the fuss?" he asked.

"It's our goose!" cried Margery. "She's vanished from her pen!"

"What's all this commotion?" asked her friend Will as he came bicycling past, so Margery told him.

"Tut!" went Will. "That'll never do," and he thought a bit while Pete and Margery thought too.

"I know," said Will. "Hop on my bike and we'll head for the stream. Perhaps she's gone for a swim."

Will held his bike while Pete and Margery hopped on behind. With a wibble and wobble, Will pedalled away. They whizzed past a man who was going fishing.

"Where are you all off to?" asked the fisherman, whose name was Bert.

"Margery and Pete's goose has disappeared," said Will to Bert.

"I'll help you look," said Bert. So with a squish and a squeeze, he pushed in between Pete and Margery.

"Pedal on, Will," they all chorused. And off went Will pedalling hard, heading for the stream.

"Tee hee!" giggled two little boys.

"Look at that bike!" sniggered Johnny to his mate Joe.

"Come along and help us," Will called out to the kids.

"The goose is missing and you can help us search," said Bert.

Johnny and Joe clambered up and balanced on Bert and Pete's shoulders.

Off went the bicycle, wibbling only slightly and wobbling quite a bit. While Will pedalled Margery looked left and Pete looked right. Bert tried to hold the boys steady, but they just giggled.

As they were reaching the stream, they saw a most peculiar thing. A big red fox was sitting, bold as brass, on a bench beside the road. With a swivel and a swerve, the bicycle party came to a halt.

"Have you seen a goosey, my love?" asked Margery.

But the big red fox just sat and licked his lips. Margery looked at the fox and the fox looked at her. He tipped back his head and gave a great big yawn.

Now just at this point, Johnny peered at the fox.

"I just saw your goose," he said.

The big red fox shut his mouth so quickly he nearly bit his tongue.

"Are you sure?" said Pete.

"Yup!" said Johnny.

"We'll see about that!" said Margery.

She squeezed herself off the bicycle and marched up to the fox.

"You've not gone and eaten our goose, have you?" she yelled.

The big red fox shook his head. But as he said, "No, of course not!", he spat out a small white feather which floated to the ground.

Margery picked it up.

"Look at this, everyone. This fox has gone and eaten our goosey!" And with that they all leapt off the bicycle and rushed at the fox.

Pete grabbed one side of him and Will the other. They forced open the fox's mouth and furious Margery stretched her arm down his neck . . . and pulled out the goose.

"We're having this for *our* tea," she said to the fox.

The poor old goose looked paler and paler.

"Hang about!" said Will. "What about the goose? We saved her to be free, not for you and Pete to have for your tea!"

Will took the goose, popped her in his bag and perched it on the front of his bike.

"I've got a better idea," he added. "Why don't you all come along with me, and I'll make something extra special for your tea."

What a grand picture they all made. Perched behind Will and the goose in the bag sat Margery and the fox, Pete, Johnny, Bert and Joe. When they got to Will's house they sat round the kitchen table and tucked into their tea of juicy nut cutlets and two veg.

And everyone was happy.

Margery found her goose.

Goose was rescued.

Fox got fed and so did Bert, Johnny, Joe and Pete.

Now they're all planning to go on a fishing trip next Saturday. And how will they get to the river? Why, by bicycle of course.

Gone Fishing

BEFORE GOLDILOCKS

Vivian French

Once upon a time there was a wood, and in the middle of the wood was a neat little house. The walls were painted white and the front door was blue, and bright red curtains fluttered at the windows.

Inside the house everyone was up and busy. Mummy Bear was cooking the porridge for breakfast. Daddy Bear was pouring milk into a jug. Baby Bear was running to and fro putting a great big spoon, a middle-sized spoon and a little teeny spoon on the table.

"What a good little bear you are," said Daddy Bear, and he patted Baby Bear on the head.

"Is my breakfast ready now?" asked Baby Bear.

"Not yet, dear," said Mummy Bear.

"Bother," said Baby Bear. He rubbed his nose, then stumped across the room and picked up the sugar bowl. "Put the sugar on the table," he said, and climbed up on his little teeny chair with the bowl in his paws.

CRASH!

Baby Bear and the sugar bowl and the little teeny chair were all in a heap on the floor. "Wah! Wah! WAAAAAAH!" howled Baby Bear.

Mummy Bear picked up Baby Bear. Daddy Bear picked up the sugar bowl and the little teeny chair.

"Dear me," said Daddy. "I think your little teeny chair is broken, Baby Bear."

Baby Bear stopped crying to look. Daddy Bear was quite right. The little teeny chair was squashed flat.

"What a shame," said Mummy Bear. "Never mind. I'm sure Daddy Bear can mend it." She put Baby Bear down and went to fetch a dustpan and brush.

"Can I sit in your great big chair, Daddy Bear?" asked Baby Bear.

Daddy nodded. "If you promise to sit still," he said.

Baby Bear climbed up into Daddy Bear's great big chair. There was a strong smell of burning porridge. Baby Bear wrinkled up his nose. "Pooh!" he said.

"Oh! Oh my goodness me!" Mummy Bear stopped sweeping up the sugar and rushed to the stove.

Baby Bear began to wriggle about in Daddy Bear's chair. He stood up, and slid down. He stood up again, and slid backwards. Then he tried with his eyes shut.

CRASH!

Baby Bear knocked the milk jug off the table.

"Baby Bear!" said Daddy Bear. "Look what you've done!"

"I didn't mean to," said Baby Bear.

"Well, sit down and don't wriggle!" said Daddy Bear.

Baby Bear sat down. Then he got up again. "Your great big chair's too hard," he said. "That's why I wriggled. It's MUCH too hard." And he climbed out of Daddy Bear's great big chair and into Mummy Bear's soft and comfy middle-sized chair.

"Is my breakfast ready yet?" he asked.

Mummy Bear was pouring the porridge into three bowls. A great big bowl, a middle-sized bowl, and a teeny little bowl.

"Here you are," she said, and she put the bowls on the table. "Now, eat it all up."

"Delicious!" said Daddy Bear. He took a great big spoonful and began to cough. "H'm," he said, and put his spoon down. "It's very – er – hot."

"I'm sure it's not, dear," said Mummy Bear. She took a middle-sized spoonful, and spluttered. "Ah," she said, and put her spoon down. "Yes," she said. "Yes. It is rather hot."

Baby Bear put his little teeny spoon into his little teeny bowl of porridge and tasted it.

"Yuck!" he said. "It's nasty!"

"Now, now, dear," said Mummy Bear. "Have a little sugar on it."

"No!" said Baby Bear. "I don't like it! I don't want porridge! I don't want porridge ever ever ever again!"

Mummy Bear and Daddy Bear stared at Baby Bear.

"But Baby Bear," Mummy Bear said, "we ALWAYS have porridge for breakfast!"

Daddy Bear nodded. "We have porridge for breakfast every day, Baby Bear. That's what bears do. Eat porridge for breakfast."

Baby Bear jumped up and down on Mummy Bear's chair. "I know we do! And I'm tired of it! I hate porridge! Wah! Wah! WAAAAH!" And he tipped his porridge onto the floor.

Mummy Bear and Daddy Bear looked at each other.

"I think," said Mummy Bear, "we should send him to bed."

"Yes," said Daddy Bear. "Baby Bears have to be good and learn to eat their porridge."

"That's right," said Mummy Bear. She picked up the howling Baby Bear. "Come along, now. Off to bed!"

Baby Bear didn't want to go to bed. He bounced on Daddy Bear's great big bed until the bedclothes fell on the floor. He rolled himself up in the blankets on Mummy Bear's middle-sized bed and piled the pillows into a heap. At last he snuggled down in his own little teeny bed and shut his eyes tightly. Daddy Bear and Mummy Bear tiptoed downstairs.

"Goodness me," said Daddy Bear.

"I think," said Mummy Bear, "I need some fresh air."

"Good idea," said Daddy Bear. "Let's go for a walk."

"Just a little walk," said Mummy Bear. "We'll be back before Baby Bear wakes up."

Daddy Bear shuffled his feet. "Do you think we should tidy up first?"

Mummy Bear looked round the kitchen. There were two steaming bowls of porridge on the table; a great big bowl and a middle-sized bowl. There was a little teeny bowl that was empty. The great big chair and the middle-sized chair were rumpled and crumpled. The little teeny chair was lying broken on the floor in among the mess of milk and sugar and porridge. Upstairs the great big bed and the middle-sized bed were most untidy . . . but at least Baby Bear was fast asleep in the little teeny bed.

"We'll tidy up when we get back," said Mummy Bear firmly. She sniffed. "Perhaps we'd better leave the front door open. It does smell of burnt porridge in here . . . just a little bit."

So Daddy Bear and Mummy Bear went out for their walk. When Goldilocks came up the path and knocked on the open door there wasn't any answer . . .

I like porridge for breakfast... do you?

LITTILL, TRITTILL AND THE BIRDS

Lucy Coats

Once upon a time there was a king who ruled the land at the top of the world. King Linnik's wife had died long ago, but he had a beautiful daughter. Princess Freya was not the sort of girl to shut herself away in a castle and spin and embroider and giggle with her ladies-in-waiting. She liked to walk in the streets and work in the gardens and talk to people. King Linnik was very proud of her and looked forward to the day when he could retire and leave running the kingdom to her.

One morning Freya didn't come down to breakfast. Her porridge grew cold on the table as the king sent messengers to look for her. But she was nowhere to be found.

King Linnik was in despair, but he *was* a king, and the king's job was to keep everyone cheerful in times of trouble. So he kept everyone busy searching and sent out proclamations and tried to be cheerful too. Days went by, and there was still no sign of Princess Freya, so the king offered a reward – half his kingdom and the princess's hand in marriage to any man who could bring her safely home.

Reward for the safe return of Princess Freya signed the KING

Now, not far from the palace lived an old man and his wife who had three sons. Thorn was the eldest, Josti was the middle one and Gersten was the youngest. They were very poor, for they had only a few sheep and a little corn and vegetable patch to see them through the year.

The two elder boys were tough and rough and their parents let them run around much as they liked. Poor Gersten was smaller and weaker and his brothers made him do all the work while they fished in the stream or played nine-stone bowling.

When Thorn heard about King Linnik's reward he was delighted. "A strong fellow like me is bound to succeed!" he boasted. So his parents gave him their blessing and a bag of bread and cheese and apples and he went on his way. Up hill and down dale he marched, swinging his stick, until, about mid-morning, he felt hungry and sat down on a large rock. Just as he had opened his bag of food, a little old man with a grey beard and yellow boots popped up beside him.

"Hello," said the little man, "can I have a bit?"

"Go away!" said Thorn rudely. "Or I'll make you." So the little man went away muttering crossly to himself. Then Thorn went on until he got hungry again. As he sat down under a large tree another little man jumped from behind it, this time wearing bright blue boots.

"Hello," said the little man, "can I have a bit?"

"Scat," snarled Thorn, and he picked up a stone. The second little man glared at him and stomped off.

Later on Thorn reached a waterfall. He splashed his face and sat down on the grass to finish the last of his food. At once a flock of brightly coloured birds appeared round his head, twittering for crumbs. He lashed out at them with his stick and they scattered, shrieking.

As Thorn walked on, the way became harder and more rocky. At sunset, he found himself at the mouth of the cave, filled with huge mooing cattle. He went in and there stood an enormous giantess.

"Welcome, Thorn," she boomed. "You may stay the night if you will clean out my cattle for me in the morning. If you fail, I shall punish you."

So the next morning, after the giantess had left, Thorn set to work. But the moment he touched the pitchfork it stuck to his hands and he could not move it however hard he tried. When the giantess came back she was very angry and she turned him into an ugly stone mug which she hung on the cave wall, along with several others.

When Thorn did not return, Josti decided to go and search for the princess too. His parents gave him the last of the good bread and apples and waved him on his way. But Josti did not behave any better than Thorn on his journey, nor did he have any more success with the giantess. Soon he too was an ugly mug hanging on the cave wall.

At the beginning of autumn, when he had got the harvest in, Gersten set out to look for Princess Freya himself. He took a bag of old crusts, for he did not want his mother and father to run short, and set off at dawn, whistling a happy tune. Like his brothers, he stopped at the big rock for a rest, but when the little man popped up beside him he said, "Good morning, grandfather. Would you like to share my breakfast? I'm sure this is your rock I'm sitting on."

The little man hopped up beside him and chewed on a crust. "Very nice," he said when he had finished. "I'm Littill. If you ever need help just call my name." And he disappeared.

Gersten was very tired when he reached the big tree, and he sat down with relief. At once the second little man jumped out from behind it.

"Hello, grandfather," said Gersten. "I have crusts enough for two if you'd like to share."

The little man's blue boots twinkled as he danced about eating his crusts. "Delicious," he said. "I'm Trittill. If you ever need help just call my name." And he too disappeared.

Gersten went wearily on and when he came to the waterfall he drank and drank. Soon the birds were flocking round his head expectantly.

"Oh!" he cried. "How beautiful you are!" And he threw them all the rest of his crusts. The largest bird flew onto his shoulder.

"We are your birds now," he chirped into Gersten's ear. "If you need help just call."

At the giantess's cave Gersten was so tired he would have agreed to anything, and so in the morning he found himself stuck to the pitchfork, just as his brothers had. He struggled for a bit, and then he remembered his friends.

"Littill, Trittill, come and help me!" he shouted, and at once the two little men were beside him, dancing and singing:

Pitchfork prong
and shovel clean
Up and down
and in-between!

And at once the pitchfork unstuck itself and began to tidy the stable.

When the giantess came back, Littill and Trittill had gone and Gersten was sitting outside the sparkling stable alone. The giantess looked at him closely.

"Hmmmm! I think you had a little help, but never mind. If you can do one more task for me in the morning I will give you whatever you ask for."

Gersten agreed, and at sunrise the giantess took him into her bedroom.

"My mattress is lumpy," she said. "Take all the feathers out and air them and put them back. But if there is even one missing I will do the same to you as I did to your brothers."

Gersten took the enormous mattress outside and emptied the feathers carefully into a pile in the sun. But as he did so, a little wind got up and blew all the feathers away. Gersten chased after them frantically, but he could not catch them.

"Littill, Trittill and *all* my birds," he cried, "help me now!" And at once the air was filled with birds with their beaks full of feathers, and Littill and Trittill ran towards him with large nets in which they had caught the rest. Quickly they stuffed the mattress with feathers (all except for three which Gersten tied together and hid in his pocket) and put it back on the giantess's bed.

"Thank you, my friends," panted Gersten. "What shall I ask for as my reward?"

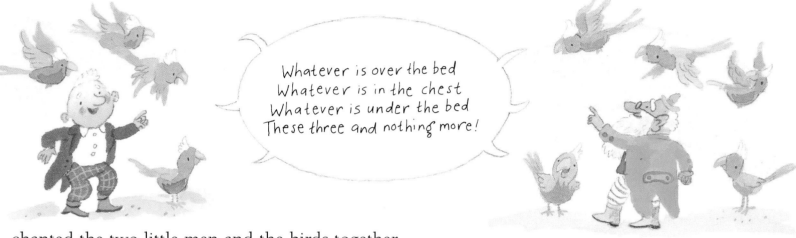

Whatever is over the bed
Whatever is in the chest
Whatever is under the bed
These three and nothing more!

chanted the two little men and the birds together.

When the giantess returned she went straight into the cave and lay down on her bed.

"Aahaa!" she roared. "There are three feathers missing!" But Gersten ran up and tickled her under the nose with the three feathers he had in his pocket, and gave them to her.

"Oh, Gersten, Gersten," she sighed when she had finished laughing, "you had help. But I keep my word. What would you like as your reward?"

Whatever is over the bed
Whatever is in the chest
Whatever is under the bed
These three and nothing more!

said Gersten.

215

"Nothing more!" said the giantess. "Why, you have ruined me as it is, boy!" And with that she pressed a secret catch and opened a door in the rock above the bed. Out stepped Princess Freya, who ran to Gersten and hugged him. Next, the giantess opened the lid of the chest to show them a fortune in gold and pearls and jewels, and then she slung it on her back and beckoned them to follow her down the secret stairway under the bed. At the bottom of the stairs was the sea and there, anchored close by, lay a beautiful magical ship which would take them wherever they wished. Gersten loaded the chest onto the ship and then he and the princess asked it to take them home.

Gersten and Freya got married the next spring, and the whole country turned out to throw rose petals at them, including King Linnik and Gersten's parents. Everybody lived happily ever after except for Thorn and Josti, who spent the rest of their lives herding cows for the giantess.

# The Twins and the Wet, Wet, Wet

Alan Gibbons

At first the twins didn't like the wet, wet, wet.

It was too wet, wet, wet.

"Can we go to a park?" asked Rachel.

"Too wet," said Dad, pointing out of the window at the pouring rain.

"Can we go to town?" asked Megan.

"Too wet," said Mum. "Just listen to that rain."

And the twins listened. To the drip, drip, drip of the wet, wet, wet.

They were stuck in. They watched a video until they got bored. They played with their dolls. But they got bored with that too. And that's when they remembered the wet, wet, wet. Not outside where it was raining. Inside where it came out of the tap.

They went into the bathroom.

"Where are you, girls?" called Dad.

"Upstairs," said Rachel.

"What are you doing?" asked Mum.

"Just playing," said Megan.

And it was true. They were. Just playing with the wet, wet, wet.

Rachel turned on the hot tap, being very careful not to touch the water, and Megan turned on the cold tap. Then they watched as it swirled down the plughole.

"We could play boats," said Rachel.

"If we put in the plug," said Megan.

So they did.

"Dinner's nearly ready," said Dad.

"Uh huh," said Rachel.

"Is cheese on toast OK?" asked Mum.

"Uh huh," said Megan.

The twins didn't care what was for dinner. They were watching the wet, wet, wet.

"It's filling up," said Rachel.

"Filling up fast," said Megan.

Too fast. It reached the overflow.

"Oh oh," cried Rachel.

Too fast. It reached the edge of the sink.

"Oh oh," cried Megan.

Too fast. It started spilling over. Onto the floor. Making the carpet wet, wet, wet.

"Turn it off," wailed Rachel.

But the taps wouldn't turn. They were stuck.

"Let's tell," said Megan.

So they ran. The twins. Away from the wet, wet, wet.

But they didn't need to tell. Downstairs Mum and Dad were about to find out for themselves.

"What's that?" asked Dad with a frown.

He'd noticed the drip, drip, drip of the wet, wet, wet. Down from the ceiling and onto the kitchen table.

"It's water," said Mum, and up they both looked.

At the drip, drip, drip of the wet, wet, wet.

"The twins!" they cried together.

And who should arrive at that very moment? The twins, of course.

"It's the water," cried Rachel.

"It won't stop," cried Megan.

Dad flew upstairs and turned off the taps. He didn't look happy.

Mum stood on the bathroom carpet and felt the squelch, squelch, squelch of the wet, wet, wet. She wasn't happy either.

"Don't you ever . . ." said Dad.
"Ever . . ." said Mum.
"Ever do that again!"
they said together.

The twins remembered the drip, drip, drip and the squelch, squelch, squelch of the wet, wet, wet.

"Never," said Rachel.

"Never," said Megan.

And they didn't. At least, not for a while.

THE TOPSY-TURVIES

Francesca Simon

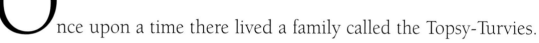

Once upon a time there lived a family called the Topsy-Turvies.

The Topsy-Turvies always got up at midnight. They put on their pyjamas, then went upstairs and had dinner.

"Eat up, Minx," said Mr Topsy-Turvy. Minx juggled with the sausages.

"Clever girl!" said Mr Topsy-Turvy.

"Jinx, stop eating with your fork," said Mrs Topsy-Turvy. "You know that's for combing your hair. Please use your fingers and toes."

"Could you pass the jam please, Minx?" said Mr Topsy-Turvy. Minx dipped her fingers in the jar and hurled the jam at her father.

"Thanks," said Mr Topsy-Turvy.

"Could you pass the whipped cream please, Jinx?" said Mrs Topsy-Turvy. Jinx flung a handful of cream at his mother.

"Thanks, dear," said Mrs Topsy-Turvy.

221

Then it was time for school. After school they went to the park. Then they played beautiful music together and watched TV. Afterwards they ate breakfast, then it was bathtime, and then they all went to bed.

Every night and day at the Topsy-Turvies was exactly the same, until one afternoon a loud knocking at the door woke them up.

"Who can that be at this time of day?" yawned Mrs Topsy-Turvy.

It was their neighbour, Mrs Plum.

"Oh dear," said Mrs Plum. "Were you just leaving?"

"No," said Mrs Topsy-Turvy. "Why would I go outside wearing my coat?"

"I'm sorry to bother you," said Mrs Plum. "But I have to go out. Could you come over and look after little Lucy? She's as good as gold."

Mrs Topsy-Turvy was very sleepy, but she liked helping others.

"Of course," said Mrs Topsy-Turvy. "We'll be undressed in a minute."

As soon as everyone was ready, they went next door to Mrs Plum's house.

"Thank you so much," said Mrs Plum. "Do make yourselves at home and have something to eat." And off she went.

"Mum, why is Mrs Plum wearing clothes *outside*?" said Minx.

"Shh," said Mrs Topsy-Turvy. "Everyone's different."

The Topsy-Turvies goggled at Mrs Plum's house. Nothing looked right.

"Poor Mrs Plum," said Mrs Topsy-Turvey. "Let's make the house lovely for her."

The Topsy-Turvies went to work. They fixed, they fussed, and they put the house in apple-pie order.

"That's better," said Mr Topsy-Turvy.

"Careful, Lucy, don't put that apron on, you'll get paint all over it," said Mr Topsy-Turvy.

"Lucy! Don't draw on the paper!" said Mrs Topsy-Turvy. "Draw on the walls!"

"Isn't she naughty!" said Minx.

"Not everyone can be as well behaved as you, dear," said Mrs Topsy-Turvy. "Lucy, what a lovely picture!"

"I'm hungry," said Jinx.

"So am I," said Minx.

Mrs Topsy-Turvy looked at the clock. It was already five.

"We might as well have breakfast," said Mrs Topsy-Turvy. "Let's see what we can find in the bedroom."

It took them a very long time to find where Mrs Plum kept her food.

"What an odd house," said Mr Topsy-Turvy.

"How funny to eat in the kitchen," said Minx.

"Breakfast is under the table," said Mrs Topsy-Turvy. "Don't forget to wash your feet."

"What's for dessert?" said Jinx.

"Tomatoes," said Mr Topsy-Turvy.

"Yippee!" said Jinx.

"But no tomatoes until you finish your cake."

"Do I have to eat all of my cake?" said Jinx.

"Yes," said Mrs Topsy-Turvy.

Suddenly there was a noise at the window. It was a burglar.

"Hurray! We've got a visitor!" shouted Minx.

"And he's coming through the window!" said Jinx.

"Let's make everything lovely for our guest," said Mrs Topsy-Turvy.

"Please have something to eat," said Mr Topsy-Turvy, throwing tomatoes at the burglar. The burglar looked unhappy.

"Have some cake!" said Jinx, hurling his leftovers.

"No, have some of mine!" shouted Minx.

"Mine, too!" shouted Lucy.

The frightened burglar escaped as fast as he could.

"Why did he run off?" said Minx.

"I don't know," said Mr Topsy-Turvy.

Then Mrs Plum ran into the kitchen.

"Is everything all right?" said Mrs Plum. "I just saw a burglar jump out of the window!"

"Everything's fine," said Mr Topsy-Turvy.

"You chased away a burglar!" said Mrs Plum. "Thank you so much. Goodness, what a mess he made!"

"What mess?" said Mrs Topsy-Turvy.

The Topsy-Turvies waved goodbye and went home.

"Mrs Plum should have said thank you for making her house so lovely," said Minx.

"Never mind," said Mr Topsy-Turvy. "It takes all sorts to make a world."

WOLFMAN

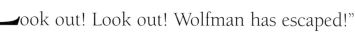

Michael Rosen

"Look out! Look out! Wolfman has escaped!"

People were running down the street screaming.

They were right.

Wolfman had broken out of his cage and now he was roaring and rampaging around town.

Everyone was rushing to get indoors.

They were terrified.

Outside, Wolfman was ripping up paving stones, biting through trees and eating lamp-posts.

It was unbelievably horrible.

The Prime Minister said, "Send in the army!"

But the army sent back a message: "Sorry, we can't. We're too scared."

Things were looking bad. Wolfman was heading down Coppers Road. People were looking out from behind their curtains thinking: please, please, please don't come near our house, Wolfman.

But Wolfman marched on.

227

Where was he going?

To the park? To the swimming pool? No.

People could see that he was heading for the house where the chief of police lived. And the chief of police was in the back room, hiding behind the armchair.

Wolfman marched on.

Nearer and nearer to the house of the chief of police.

Stomp, stomp, stomp, the ground was shaking.

"Please, please, please go away, Wolfman," whimpered the chief of police.

But Wolfman didn't stop.

He got to the garden gate in front of the chief of police's house.

Wham! He kicked it over.

Up the garden path – stomp, stomp, stomp.

Up to the door.

"Help, help, help!" screamed the chief of police from behind the door.

Wolfman slowly bent down and looked through the letterbox.

The chief of police looked up and saw Wolfman's eyes.

"What do you want, Wolfman?" called out the chief of police. "Just say! What do you want?"

There was a moment's silence.

And then, in a little moany voice, Wolfman said,

QUACKY DUCK

Paul and Emma Rogers

Once upon a pond there lived a duck who was very fond of quacking.

She quacked at the tractor. She quacked at the cat. She quacked at the farmer's funny old hat. She quacked at the heron. She quacked at the fly. She quacked at the drake who went waddling by. She quacked at the clouds. She quacked at the sun. She quacked at everything and everyone.

For when she quacked, she was happy. And when she was happy, she quacked.

"Give us a break!" said Dragonfly.

"Quack!" said Duck. "Quack! Quack!"

Dragonfly darted away over the pond.

"Couldn't we have a little peace?" complained Frog.

"Quack!" said Duck. "Quack! Quack! Quack!"

Frog flopped into the pond.

"Just a touch of silence from time to time?" said Very Old Goldfish.

"Quack!" said Duck. "Quack! Quack! Quack! Quack! Quack! Quack! Quack!"

Quack, quack! What a quacky story!

Very Old Goldfish dived down to the depths of the pond.

Duck didn't stop quacking until it was night. Then she went paddling off into the bulrushes.

Next morning on the pond, something was different. The flies buzzed, the reeds whispered – but there was no quacking. Duck had disappeared!

"Ah, that's better!" said Very Old Goldfish.

"What a lovely silence!" said Dragonfly.

"Peace at last!" said Frog.

For four whole weeks Duck was nowhere to be seen.

"It's a bit quiet without her," said Dragonfly.

"It's not the same," said Very Old Goldfish.

"A bit too peaceful," said Frog.

Then – one lazy, hazy afternoon, when Very Old Goldfish was sunning himself in the shallows, and Frog was snoozing on a log and Dragonfly was zipping amongst the shadows – there was a rustling in the bulrushes.

"QUACK!" cried Duck.

Ten little ducklings came hurrying out.

"Aha!" said the heron.

"She's back!" said the cat.

"Well," said the farmer, "just look at that!"

And everyone lived quackily every after.

THE
LITTLE WITCH

Margaret Mahy

The big city was dark. Even the streetlights were out. All day people had gone up and down, up and down; cars and trams and buses had roared and rattled busily along. But now they had all gone home to bed, and only the wind, the shadows, and a small kitten wandered in the wide, still streets.

The kitten chased a piece of paper, pretending it was a mouse. He patted at it with his paws and it flipped behind a rubbish bin. Quick as a wink he leapt after it, and then forgot it because he had found something else.

"What is this?" he asked the wind. "Here asleep behind the rubbish bin. I have never seen it before."

The wind was bowling a newspaper along, but he dropped it and came to see. The great stalking shadows looked down from everywhere.

"Ah," said the wind, "it is a witch . . . see her broomstick . . . but she is only a very small one."

The wind was right. It was a very small witch – a baby one.

The little witch heard the wind in her sleep and opened her eyes. Suddenly she was awake.

Far above, the birds peered down at the street below.

"Look!" said the shadows to the sparrows under the eaves. "Look at the little witch; she is such a little witch to be all alone."

"Let me see!" a baby sparrow peeped sleepily.

"Go to sleep!" said his mother. "I didn't hatch you out of the egg to peer at witches all night long."

She snuggled him back into her warm feathers. But there was no one to snuggle a little witch, wandering cold in the big empty streets, dragging a broom several sizes too big for her. The kitten sprang at the broom. Then he noticed something.

"Wind!" he cried. "See! – Wherever this witch walks, she leaves a trail of flowers!"

Yes, it was true! The little witch had lots of magic in her, but she had not learned to use it properly, or to hide it, any more than she had learned to talk.

So wherever she put her feet mignonette grew, and rosemary, violets, lily of the valley, and tiny pink-and-white roses . . . all through the streets, all across the road . . .

Butterflies came, from far and wide, to dance and drink.

"Who is that down there?" asked a young moth.

"It is a baby witch who has made these fine crimson feast-rooms for us," a tattered old moth answered.

The wind followed along, playing and juggling with the flowers and their sweet smells. "I shall sweep these all over the city," he said. In their sleep, people smelled the flowers and smiled, dreaming happily.

Now the witch looked up at the tall buildings; windows looked down at her with scorn, and their square sharp shapes seemed angry to her. She pointed her finger at them.

Out of the cracks and chinks suddenly crept long twining vines and green leaves. Slowly flowers opened on them . . . great crimson flowers like roses, smelling of honey.

The little witch laughed, but in a moment she became solemn. She was so alone. Then the kitten scuttled and pounced at her bare, pink heels, and the little witch knew she had a friend. Dragging her broom for the kitten to chase, she wandered on, leaving a trail of flowers.

Now the little witch stood in the street, very small and lost, and cold in her blue smock and bare feet.

She pointed up at the city clock tower and it became a huge fir tree, while the clock face turned into a white nodding owl and flew away!

The owl flew as fast as the wind to a tall dark castle perched high on a hill. There at the window sat a slim, tired witch-woman, looking out into the night. "Where, oh where is my little baby witch? I must go and search for her again."

"Whoo! Whoo!" cried the owl. "There is a little witch down in the city and she is enchanting everything. What will the people say tomorrow?"

The witch-woman rode her broomstick through the sky and over the city, looking eagerly down through the mists. Far below she could see the little witch running and hiding in doorways, while the kitten chased after her.

Down flew the witch-woman – down, down to a shop doorway. The little witch and the kitten stopped and stared at her.

"Why," said the witch-woman, in her dark, velvety voice, "you are my own dear little witch . . . my little lost witch!" She held out her arms and the little witch ran into them. She wasn't lost any more.

The witch-woman looked around at the enchanted city, and she smiled. "I'll leave it as it is," she said, "for a surprise tomorrow."

Then she gathered the little witch onto her broomstick, and the kitten jumped on, too, and off they went to their tall castle home, with windows as deep as night, and lived there happily ever after.

And the next day when the people got up and came out to work, the city was full of flowers and the echoes of laughter.

THE SELFISH GIANT

Oscar Wilde

retold by *Lucy Coats*

Far away and long ago there was a land called Lyonesse, where fairies still danced in the forests, and witches and wolves were as common as clouds in the sky. Right in the middle of Lyonesse, huddled under the chalk downs, was the little town of Sheepcote. Sheepcote people were busy and hardworking, and although they loved their children, they didn't have much time to play with them, and tended to shout if they got in the way. So the children played with each other in a great gang that rampaged around the woods and fields, and got into mischief.

One sunny day at the beginning of summer, the children were roaming further afield than usual when they came to a beautiful garden. It was a perfect playground with low trees to climb, and streams to build dams in, ripe fruit to eat when they were hungry, and flowers to pick when they weren't. Best of all, there were no grown-ups to shout at them, not even in the big castle at the centre of the garden. The children went there each day for the rest of that summer, and all through the autumn and winter. Though the leaves dropped from the trees, and the flowers slipped back into the earth, it was never cold, and even the rabbits and foxes and birds became their friends in the magical place.

But one day, towards the end of winter, as the children went into the garden they heard a great voice roaring at them.

"OUT! OUT! OUT!" the voice shouted. "How dare you come into my garden? It's my garden, mine! Mine! Mine! Not for anyone else! GO AWAY!" And coming towards them the children saw a huge and horrible giant, waving his enormous arms, and shaking his enormous fists, and stomping his gigantic boots so that the earth trembled. The children fled terrified, and so did the rabbits and foxes and birds and even the worms and insects so that there was nothing and nobody left in the garden except for the giant.

He had been away up in the North Country for seven times seven long years, counting and counting his hoards of treasure and not spending a penny of it on anyone except himself. Cursing and muttering, the giant immediately set about building a high wall all the way around his garden so that nobody else should enjoy it except for him. He stuck up notices which said:

 and  and

He was a *very* selfish giant.

Although it was the end of winter when the giant came back, April and May and June came and went, and still spring would not return to the garden. She thought the giant was just too selfish. No birds sang, and the trees hung lifeless and sad and cold, while just over the wall crocuses and primroses appeared and the seasons turned as usual. Jack Frost came to visit the garden, and froze the water in the streams and ponds. He liked it so much that he invited his sister Snow and his brother Hail to stay. Snow appeared in the night and spread her beautiful white cloak everywhere. The giant looked gloomily out of his window and shivered as Hail threw himself about on the roof and laughed as the castle tiles broke and smashed on the hard ground beneath.

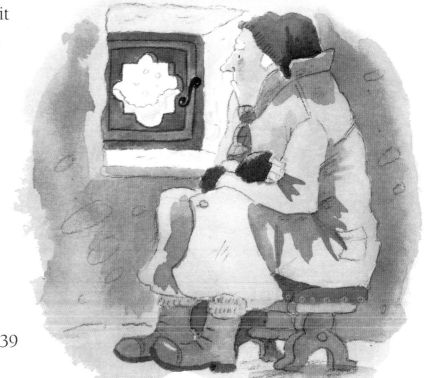

239

Nothing changed in the garden except that the snow got deeper and deeper, more and more tiles and then windows got broken, and the frost crept into the bricks and mortar of the high wall and crumbled them away. The giant's nose turned blue and dripped and he caught a giant-sized cold which made him sneeze till the whole castle shook. Sometimes he cursed spring for not appearing, sometimes he shouted names at the banished children, but mostly he sat and brooded and wrapped himself in more blankets. Never – not once – did he blame himself. He was stupid as well as selfish.

One day, about a year after his return, the giant was sitting in bed feeling sorry for himself when he heard a beautiful sound. On his snowy windowsill a blackbird blinked its orange eye at him and opened its beak to let a ripple of notes flow out into the air. The giant lifted his nose and sniffed. He could smell a wonderful smell – a smell of warm damp earth, and green things growing and . . . a smell of SPRING!

The giant felt a strange feeling in his chest as he ran down the stairs and flung open the castle doors. He looked across the garden, and saw that the snow had disappeared and that there were children sitting in every tree, and that all the trees were covered in wonderful pink and white blossom.

Only in one small corner of the garden was it still winter, and in that corner stood a boy, crying as if he would never stop. He was too small to climb up into the lower branches of the tree he had chosen, and Snow and Hail were whirling and dancing above it, and taunting him. In that moment, the giant's heart opened as he understood how selfish and stupid he had been, and he ran towards the child to help him.

241

As the other children heard the giant coming, they scrambled down and away through the gap in the wall which Jack Frost had made, and immediately the garden was deep in winter again. But the little boy was crying so loudly that he never heard the giant, and soon he felt himself being lifted up by gentle hands, and set on the lowest branch of the tree, which burst into flower at once.

He looked into the giant's eyes and smiled bravely, and the giant smiled too and he took out a large clean white handkerchief, and wiped the little boy's eyes and nose, and then the little boy kissed him. The giant had never been kissed before, and he rather liked it. The last of his selfishness melted away like the snow, and he walked away from the little boy to fetch a sledgehammer from his toolshed to knock down the high wall and an axe to chop down all the notices around it.

When the other children saw what the giant was doing, they crept into the garden again.

The sun shone out as they entered and the grass and leaves and flowers grew and blossomed as if they wanted to make one day do for ten. The giant worked his way steadily round the wall, and when he had knocked the last brick down he crouched down in front of the children and said, "This is your garden now, children. You can play in it for ever and ever."

Then he looked round for the child who had kissed him, but he was nowhere to be seen. The giant asked the children where he was, but they didn't seem to know him, and although the giant searched high and low, the little boy was not anywhere in the garden.

The giant was sad for a while, but he cheered up when the other children let him join in their games, and soon his memories of the little boy faded. The years passed, and the children grew up and married each other and went to work in Sheepcote or in other places in the land of Lyonesse. But however hardworking and busy they became, they never quite forgot the magic of the giant's garden, and when their own children came along they played with them a little more and worked a little less and shouted at them as little as possible. Many children still went to the giant's garden, but as time went by he became very old and too stiff to run about with them any more, so he sat in his enormous deck chair under a tree, and smiled sleepily as he watched them instead.

Very early one morning, as the giant was waiting for the children to arrive, he noticed a door in the hedge that he had never seen before. He pulled himself creakily to his feet, walked over to it and pushed it open. There on the other side was the little boy he had loved so long ago. With a glad cry the giant dropped to his knees and held his arms out wide and the little boy ran into them laughing.

"Come and play in my garden now," said the little boy, and they walked off together into the spring sunshine.

When the children came into the giant's garden later that morning, his deck chair was all filled with spring blossoms although it was the end of summer. The hedge had no sign of any door, and the giant was gone as if he had never been.

OLLY'S FLYING LESSON

Georgie Adams

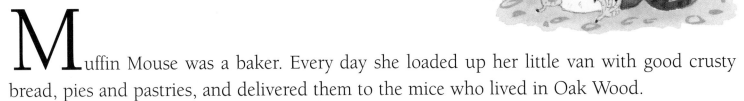

Muffin Mouse was a baker. Every day she loaded up her little van with good crusty bread, pies and pastries, and delivered them to the mice who lived in Oak Wood.

One spring morning, Muffin was driving along Loopy Lane. The trees in Oak Wood were bursting with new leaves and the birds were busy feeding their young. But as Muffin's van rattled round a bend, she saw something sitting in the road.

Muffin tooted her horn, but whatever it was didn't move. So she stopped the van and got out. Muffin peered at a scraggy ball of feathers. And as she looked close, two large eyes opened and blinked. An owl, who was not very old, had fallen out of its nest!

"I'm Muffin," said Muffin.

"I'm Olly," said the little owl.

"Well, Olly," said Muffin, gently. "You can't stay here. Come with me. I'll look after you."

So Olly went to live with Muffin, and the two became very good friends.

One windy afternoon when Muffin had finished baking, Olly began flying lessons. First, he had to learn how to take off. Olly stood on the roof of the van, while Muffin called out instructions below.

246

Wake up, Olly! Don't go to sleep before the story's finished!

"One, two, three . . . jump!" she shouted. "Now flap! Keep flapping!"

Olly flapped his wings. But the wind blew him sideways, and he landed upside down at Muffin's feet.

"How did I do?" asked Olly, looking dazed.

"A good start," said Muffin thoughtfully, and she disappeared inside her house. A few minutes later she came out with an armful of cushions. She spread the cushions on the grass.

"Try again," she said, "and aim for these."

Bravely, Olly launched himself off the roof. Only this time, he was flapping so fast, he missed the cushions and bumped his beak on a tree. Which was very painful.

"I'll never learn to fly properly," sniffed Olly.

"Of course you will," said Muffin, giving him a cuddle. "Just keep at it and you'll get there. Which reminds me of a story," she said.

"Ooo," said Olly, wiping his tears away. "I love stories!"

So the flying lesson stopped, while Muffin told him this story . . .

"One day, Hare met Tortoise on the road to a farm," she began. *"There was a barn full of apples at the farm, and the two were looking forward to a feast.*

On the way, Hare boasted about how fast he could run. Unlike Tortoise, who moved so slowly. 'I'll be surprised if you ever get to the farm at all!' said Hare.

'Slow and steady, that's me,' said Tortoise. 'Still, I'm sure I could race you to the barn.'

Hare burst out laughing. 'You race me!' he said. 'Right. On your marks. Get set. Go!'

So the two animals set off, each at their own pace. The Hare leapt away down the road, leaving Tortoise crawling behind. In no time at all, he was well ahead.

The day was hot and sunny, and soon Hare began to feel sleepy. He looked down the road. He could just see Tortoise in the distance.

'Old slowcoach!' said Hare to himself. 'There's plenty of time for a nap.' So he sat down under a tree and fell asleep.

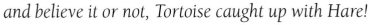
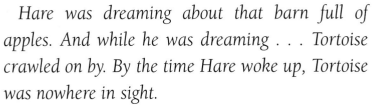

Meanwhile Tortoise was making her way slowly, but surely. The sun was warm on her shell and the bees were humming. But she didn't stop. Not for a minute. She just kept on going and believe it or not, Tortoise caught up with Hare!

Hare was dreaming about that barn full of apples. And while he was dreaming . . . Tortoise crawled on by. By the time Hare woke up, Tortoise was nowhere in sight.

Well, you should have seen him run! Hare ran as fast as his long legs could carry him so that the wind whistled past his ears. But he was too late! Hare came dashing into the farmyard, to find Tortoise waiting for him.

'Slow and steady, that's me,' said Tortoise. 'And I've won the race!'

248

"And that," said Muffin, "is the end of the story."

"It was a good story," said Olly. "I never thought Tortoise would win."

"It's amazing what you can do if you keep trying," said Muffin. "And, talking of trying . . . how about another flying lesson?"

"Just watch me!" said Olly.

And before bedtime that evening . . . Olly was flying!

"I knew you could do it," said Muffin, as she tucked Olly into bed that night.

"I'll fly to the Big Oak tomorrow," said Olly sleepily.

"And back again, I hope!" said Muffin.

But there was no answer from the little owl because . . . Olly was fast asleep!

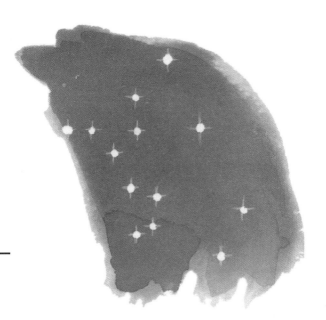

STAIRWAY TO THE STARS

Mary Hoffman

There was once a little girl who wanted the stars to play with. Every night she looked out of her bedroom window and thought they looked so bright and sparkly she would like to have them for a game of marbles or to make a necklace with.

One day she decided to set out to find the stars. She asked everyone she met until at last she caught up with the Good Folk, dancing on the grass. "Have you seen the stars in the sky?" she asked. "For I'd dearly love some to play with."

"Why," said the Good Folk, "we often see them shining on the grass while we dance. Dance with us and you may see them too."

So the little girl danced till she was warm as toast, but she didn't see any stars. Then one of the Good Folk said, "If you really want to reach the stars, you must get Four Feet to carry you, then No Feet, and then you must climb the stairway without steps . . ."

The little girl hurried away and soon she came to where a horse was tied to a tree. "You must be Four Feet," she said. "The Good Folk say you must carry me to No Feet, because I am on my way to the stars!"

The horse obeyed and carried her out of the woods and down to the wild seashore. On the water was a wide silver path leading to a glowing arch of many colours.

"This is as far as I go," said the horse and the little girl got down. A big fish swam right up to her at the water's edge. "Are you No Feet?" she asked. "The Good Folk sent me here on Four Feet and I am on my way to the stars."

"Get on my back and hold tight," said the fish. The little girl clung on and the fish swam through the water along the wide silver path to the coloured arch. When they reached it, he said, "There's your way. You have to climb the arch if you can."

"The stairway to the stars at last!" thought the little girl, and she started to climb. But it was really hard. There were no steps and it was so shiny bright that the little girl got dazzled and dizzy. And the higher she climbed, the more she felt she was falling. She climbed and she climbed into the freezing starlight till she was shivering with fear and cold and at last she could hang on no longer and she let go.

She came to with a bang on the bare boards by her bed at home, with the starlight streaming through her window and the tears streaming down her face. And she never knew if she would have had the stars to play with if she had managed to hang on a bit longer.

That's all! Did you like those stories? Frog, Mouse and Duck have had a lovely time telling them, but now it's time for the picnic. They're hungry!

Who else has come to join in? Do you know who everyone is?
You will if you listened carefully! Come on, let's go and enjoy the picnic before it's time for another story.

Acknowledgements

Olly's Flying Lesson © Georgie Adams 1998; *The Little Girl and the Tiny Doll* © Aingelda and Edward Ardizzone 1966, first published by Longman Young Books/Viking; *Piggo and the Pony* and *Piggo Has a Train Ride* © Pam Ayres 1998; *A Name for Nettie, Nettie's New House* and *Nettie's New Shoes* © Lynda Britnell 1996, first published by Orion Children's Books; *Wonderful Woody* and *Woof's Worst Day* © Patricia Cleveland-Peck 1998; *Littill, Trittill and the Birds, The Selfish Giant* and *The Tinderbox* © Lucy Coats 1998; *Doctor Boox and the Sore Giraffe* © Andrew Davies 1972, first published by William Collins & Sons Ltd in *The Fantastic Feats of Doctor Boox*; *Fussy* and *How to Read in the Dark* © Anne Fine 1998; *The Two Giants* © Michael Foreman 1967, first published by Hodder & Stoughton's Children's Books; *Before Goldilocks, Goldilocks and the Three Bears, Huffing and Puffing, The Three Billy Goats Gruff, The Three Little Pigs and the Big Bad Wolf* and *The Troll's Story* © Vivian French 1998; *Playing Princesses* © Adèle Geras 1998; *The Twins and the Wet, Wet, Wet* © Alan Gibbons 1998; *One Night I'm Going to Catch You* © Joy Haney 1998; *Stairway to the Stars* © Mary Hoffman 1998; *Crocodile Tears* and *How the Wizard's Hat Became* © Sue Inman 1998; *The Cat and the Mermaid* © Shirley Isherwood 1998; *FlowerPotamus, Flying Felix* and *How the Rabbit Got His Hop* © Michael Lawrence 1998; *Felix and the Dragon* © Angela McAllister 1993, first published by Orion Children's Books; *The Little Witch* © Margaret Mahy 1976, first published by JM Dent & Sons in *A Lion in the Meadow and 5 other favourites*; *The Rare Spotted Birthday Party* © Margaret Mahy 1984, first published by JM Dent & Sons in *Leaf Magic and 5 other favourites*; *The Strange Egg* © Margaret Mahy 1987, first published by JM Dent & Sons in *The First Margaret Mahy Storybook*; *Miranda the Castaway* © James Mayhew 1996, first published by Orion Children's Books; *Billy, the Unbelievably Greedy Baby* and *Rory, the Deplorably Noisy Baby* © Paul and Emma Rogers 1990, first published by JM Dent & Sons in *Amazing Babies*; *Quacky Duck* © Paul and Emma Rogers 1995, first published by Orion Children's Books; *Wolfman* © Michael Rosen 1998; *Horrid Henry* © Francesca Simon 1994, first published by Orion Children's Books in *Horrid Henry and Other Stories*; *The Topsy-Turvies* © Francesca Simon 1995, first published by Orion Children's Books; *Tool Trouble at Smallbills Garage* and *Alfie Makes a Splash* © Willy Smax 1994, first published by Orion Children's Books in *Benny the Breakdown Truck*; *Morton at the Building Site* © Willy Smax 1995, first published by Orion Children's Books in *Jack Tractor*; *Lottie's Letter* © Gordon Snell 1996, first published by Orion Children's Books. Every effort has been made to trace copyright holders and the publishers apologize for any inadvertent omissions.

256